CHARGE T

Nick Ryan

A World War 3 Technothriller Action Event

Dedication:

This book is dedicated to my fiancé, Ebony; the love of my life and my best friend.

-Nick.

The Invasion of Poland

World War III came suddenly and with fearful fury to Europe.

The early days of the conflict were a nightmare of shock and horror. While a disbelieving world watched on, Russian tanks and troops stormed across the borders of the Baltic States in their thousands. Paratroopers and fighter bombers filled the sky. The sound of artillery shattered the brittle peace and rang like the drums of doom, lighting the horizon with flashes of fire and thunder.

Estonia, Latvia and Lithuania were overwhelmed, assaulted on every front by well coordinated Russian strikes. NATO troops spread thin across the Baltics were quickly crushed. Within days the invading Russian army was well-established and fortifying the ground it had won, while stubborn resistance fighters battled on to their inevitable bitter end.

NATO reeled from the conflict, appalled and stunned. The combined Russian assault into the Baltics was so overpowering that for several days the allied armies were flung back in disarray. Diplomatic protests went unheard. The death toll reached tragic proportions. Towns and cities were reduced to rubble. Crumpled corpses lay bloated and broken amidst the ruins. The sky filled with a black pall of smoke that hung over all of Europe.

Not content with the ground gains won during their brutal *gromovaya voyna* 'thunder war', the Russian generals cast their covetous gaze southwards to a narrow stretch of land between the Russian exclave of Kaliningrad and the border of Belarus.

Punching through the Suwalki Gap with an iron fist of armor, beneath a swarm of fighter jets and a barrage of missiles, the Russian Army burst through NATO's ragged border defenses and drove deep into Poland.

One by one, towns in the northeast of the country fell to the relentless advance of steel and soldiers until the tip of the Russian spear was within one hundred kilometers of Warsaw.

Defending their advance were a ramshackle assortment of hastily-assembled NATO troops, under-equipped and ill-prepared – while on the flanks of the spearhead allied units sought to contest the Russian advance through a series of lightning attacks and precision air strikes.

It was a time of killing and chaos.

It was a time of dark despair and fear.

And it was a time when even the best and bravest of soldiers had to fight with savage desperation just for the right to survive...

Chapter 1:

The sound of clattering steel tracks mixed with the roar of diesel engines as the vehicles turned off Tadeusza Kosciuszki and then swung southeast. They were Polish Army BMP-1 armored troop carriers, their low-profile conical turrets turning slowly from side to side through an arc of forty-five degrees as they cruised along the tree-lined street. Their uniformed vehicle commanders stood waist-high behind the open hatch covers. Wearing headsets and helmets, they stared straight ahead, their expressions stern.

The vehicles were streaked in swathes of green and brown camouflage, their grinding tracked wheels caked in clumps of dry mud. They left in their wake an oily black belch of diesel exhaust that hung in the still dawn air.

Then came the tanks; Polish PT-91 Twardy main battle tanks – vast hulking steel beasts – with their long barrels swaddled in burlap strapping to disguise their shape, and the rumbling roar of their huge engines like the sound of a rolling thunder storm.

Finally, a procession of troop-carrying trucks rounded the village corner. They were boxy Star 1466 utilities, their cargo bodies covered by paint-streaked tarpaulins to conceal the infantry they carried. They rumbled through the intersection, driven nose-to-tail.

Thirty minutes later the sky over the tiny village filled with more dreadful clattering noise. Now it was the deafening hammer of helicopter rotors beating the air that drew the villagers curiously back onto the narrow sidewalks.

The helicopters were US Army CH-47 Chinooks; huge ungainly tandem-rotor workhorses that looked like prehistoric insects against the high clouds. The Chinooks appeared from behind a tall palisade of trees to the north, their noses angled down as they streaked across the sky in pursuit of the armored column.

At the Bemowo Piskie Training Area a few miles north of Drygaly village, Sergeant First Class Tom Edge watched the last of the CH-47 Chinooks lift into the air and then he turned his attention back to the ACU jacket in his hands.

There was a bullet hole in the sleeve. He thrust his finger through the ragged tear and shook his head in wonder. He tossed the jacket to his vehicle's Scout Team Leader, Sergeant Waddingham (E-5), who held the garment up to the light to inspect it.

"You gonna sew that up, or leave it as a memento?"

Edge grunted. The bullet hole had missed the Velcro Cavalry SSI on his left sleeve by a couple of inches. He shrugged the jacket back on.

"A bit to the left and you'd be washing out blood stains."

Edge nodded. The startled Russian soldier who had stumbled onto their OP had almost killed him, his AK-74M assault rifle swinging towards Edge's center mass when Waddingham's bullet had torn the top off the man's head and sprayed the contents of his skull across the forest foliage.

"Did I ever thank you for saving my ass?"

"It was my pleasure."

Edge's team had spent the last four days conducting roadside reconnaissance from a camouflaged observation post situated three miles inside the Russian Oblast of Kaliningrad. The OP had been located on road 27A-028, east of Zheleznodorozhny, set back from the verge amidst tall trees and dense bushland. Their task had been to monitor Russian military vehicle movements.

The squad had left their Stryker M1126 and the vehicle's crew on the Polish side of the border and trekked into enemy territory in the dead of night, surviving on MRE's and broken sleep for ninety-six hours before a Russian army transport truck had stopped by the side of the road and a dozen armed soldiers had jumped down from the tarpaulin-covered cargo tray. The scouts in their hide had immediately tensed. Each man in the team had completed a sixteen-week OSUT training course at Fort Benning, and two of the squad had deployed to Camp Buehring in the middle of the Kuwaiti desert as non-combat support. But only Tom Edge and Vince Waddingham had gone to war in Afghanistan and experienced first-hand the horror and tension of combat.

Edge ordered his men to frozen silence with curt hand signals as the Russians spread out and stepped away from the road. They had their weapons slung over their shoulders. Several of the Russians had cigarettes dangling from their mouths. Edge heard the banter of subdued voices. One of the soldiers walked towards the hide and unbuttoned his trousers.

Edge took a deep breath. Straining his neck, he saw the Russian's boots and the bottom of his fatigues, stained with mud and grass. Then the trickling sound of water and the acrid stench of warm urine filled the air. The Russian coughed up a wad of phlegm and spat it into the grass.

None of the scouts dared blink. It seemed incredible that the Russian hadn't noticed them amongst the night's shadows within a few feet of where he splashed piss on his boots.

The Russian buttoned himself up and was about to turn back to the truck. The rest of the soldiers were standing in a knot by the tailgate of the vehicle, lighting fresh cigarettes, their heads huddled close together, the planes of their faces lit into harsh angles by the small flaring firelights. Someone in the group called out a name and the soldier standing by the hide grunted.

"*Podozhdi minute,*" the man growled. He started to fasten his belt and then stopped.

The man frowned curiously, then leaned forward, reaching his hand down in the dark towards Tom Edge's face.

Edge blinked.

The Russian's expression transformed into a look of utter astonishment. His mouth fell open, and then he jumped back and began shouting.

Everything seemed to happen at once. The Russian reached for his weapon. It slid off his shoulder and into his hands, but he fired too soon, spraying a burst of bullets that churned into the soft earth. Edge felt something snatch at his arm. He exploded from the shallow ditch and seized the Russian around the waist. The soldier fired again, staggering backwards. There was a strangled sound of fear choked in the back of his throat. He swung the barrel of his AK-74 back onto Edge just as Vince Waddingham opened fire, decapitating the Russian. He fell to the ground dead behind a soft cloud of pink mist.

The night erupted into a flurry of chaos, flickering flame and bullets. The Russians fired blindly into the darkness. The Americans were calm and clinical. Within seconds the soldiers around the truck were dead.

The Cavalry scouts ghosted away into the night, falling back in disciplined bounds. They reached the Polish border just as the dawn's pale light rimmed the horizon. Now they were back at Bemowo Piskie, tired and exhausted – and puzzled because the vast NATO training facility was practically abandoned.

Waddingham handed Edge a cigarette. He was an inch shorter and a year younger than Edge with a cheerful, ready smile and a dry sense of humor. He seemed to know the SFC's mind. "Where do you reckon everyone has gone?"

Edge shrugged his shoulders. "There's a war on. Maybe everyone has mobilized towards the border."

"Maybe the Russians heard 2nd Platoon, 'Outlaw Troop' were in the area and they surrendered?" Waddingham offered a lopsided grin and a moment of levity.

"I wish."

Vince Waddingham said no more. The subject was a delicate one. Tom Edge had been due to return stateside at the end of the month to take up a scout instructor's role at Fort Benning, Georgia. His wife and infant daughter had packed up their home in Dallas and moved across the country to Columbus in anticipation of his return. Now – because of the war – those plans were on hold indefinitely. The cruel twist of fortune had soured Edge's attitude and left him brooding and sullen. Waddingham knew his Platoon Sergeant was bitter, and that the sudden change of orders had put a strain on his marriage. The war with Russia had flung the world into peril, and no one was predicting a quick resolution, not even the politicians.

A Humvee braked to a sudden halt close to the two soldiers, and a man emerged from the passenger door. He came across the empty parade ground, hobbling on crutches. He had his lower right leg encased in plaster and a grimace of discomfort wrenched across his face.

Vince Waddingham did a double-take. "It's the Lieutenant."

Edge looked up and blanched with surprise.

Lieutenant 'Brit' Parker reached the two men and stopped, balancing awkwardly. His lips were pressed tightly together. The officer waved away the men's salutes irritably.

"Dammit! Dammit to hell," the 2nd Platoon commander growled with feigned tetchiness, his accent unmistakably English. "Stop waving your bloody arms about and look at my ankle."

Parker had started his military career as a teenage recruit in the British Army, and served in the Middle East. On a training course in Florida he had met and eventually married an American woman. Two years later he joined the US Cavalry. The uniform had changed, but his peculiar accent and mannerisms remained.

Edge looked dutifully. The plaster reached all the way up to the Lieutenant's right knee.

"What did you do?" Edge felt a sudden sensation of foreboding.

"I didn't do any-bloody-thing," Parker protested, although the outburst lacked real venom. "It's your fault, Edge!"

"Mine sir?" Tom Edge asked dryly. He felt like the straight-man in a good-natured comedy act.

"Of course," Parker pulled a handkerchief from his pocket and worried his nose. "You insisted on volunteering for the OP job. I shouldn't have listened to you. I should have led the patrol myself."

Edge nodded. Behind the Lieutenant's shoulder, he caught a glimpse of Vince Waddingham grinning. "Well, if it makes you feel better, Lieutenant, we did manage to get ourselves shot at and almost killed." To confirm the veracity of his report Edge poked his finger back through the bullet hole in his sleeve.

"Well it doesn't," Parker frowned. But the twinkle of mischief went from his eyes and his tone became more fatalistic. He propped his back against the side of Edge's mud-spattered Stryker and sighed, suddenly serious. "I fell in a hole on the gunnery range yesterday," he confessed dully, and made a helpless gesture with his hands. "A little bloody ditch. The doctor says I snapped my ankle, and now they're sending me home. I'm on the next helicopter to Warsaw and then back to the States."

"Oh," Edge said. His weather-worn expression darkened. Lieutenant Parker saw the disappointment on the other man's face. Edge's last possible hope of being posted back to the States had just been broken on the wheel of more ill fortune.

Parker looked genuinely apologetic. "Tom, I'm sorry," it was the first time the Lieutenant had ever uttered Edge's Christian name, "I really am."

Edge stirred himself and shrugged off his disappointment. He gave a sour laugh that lacked any trace of humor. "Well," he grunted. "At least things can't possibly get any worse."

Which was when a column of twelve Polish KTO Rosomak infantry fighting vehicles suddenly appeared.

*

Edge watched the Polish vehicles pull up in a ragged line across the concrete pad of the parade ground. Known more commonly as a Wolverine, the armored personnel carriers were 8x8 multi-role vehicles armed with a 30mm ATK Mk 44 chain gun mounted in the turret. The vehicle was based on the Finnish Patria, and had earned a reputation across Europe for being solid and reliable. The Rosomak carried a crew of three and eight passengers – and had seen combat action in Afghanistan.

Not that any of the vehicles parked on the parade ground had been in a battle, Edge guessed. They looked brand new. Their camouflage paint was unscratched, the huge tires still factory black and shiny.

"There are a couple of small things I haven't yet mentioned," Lieutenant Parker grimaced. Edge was still frowning at the curious parade of Polish vehicles. Lieutenant Parker cleared his throat to get Edge's attention.

"You men have another mission. Something important has come up. It's an opportunity to punch back hard at the Russians, and it can't wait."

Edge shot Waddingham an ominous sideways glance. The two men had been firm friends ever since their time served in Afghanistan. They worked well together, and seemed to intuitively understand each other, even in the frantic chaos of a firefight. More than anything else they trusted each other's ability as soldiers.

Lieutenant Parker wobbled on his crutches and then his tone became serious. "First, you need to know that as of right now the Platoon is yours to command into the foreseeable future. You're in charge. HQ is sending a squad leader for the fourth Stryker."

Edge said nothing. He wasn't being promoted. He was just being expected to take on a Lieutenant's work-load and responsibilities for the same meager salary. He pushed the disgruntled thought aside and gave a cold smile.

Lieutenant Parker saw Edge's expression and ploughed on manfully.

"Second is the mission. You're going back into harm's way."

Edge and Waddingham exchanged another significant glance. The men in his squad were tired and exhausted. "When?"

"Today."

"Where?"

Lieutenant Parker pulled a map of northern Poland from his pocket and Vince Waddingham unfolded it flat on the rear ramp of the Stryker. Using the rubber-capped crutch tip as a crude pointer, Parker traced a grubby line from the Poland-Lithuania border to Warsaw.

"A massive Russian armored column has come pouring through the Suwalki Gap and is making directly for Warsaw," the Lieutenant explained. "They're advancing under the cover of fighters and they're moving fast. NATO is struggling to cobble together enough troops to defend the capital. At this stage, it's doubtful we can repulse the advance."

Edge understood. The Russians had never been known for finesse. They used their armor like a battering ram, bludgeoning anything that stood in their way until they steamrolled to their objective. They had fought in the same manner for over a hundred years.

"So headquarters has come up with two immediate priorities. The first is to slow the Russian attack, giving us more time to defend Warsaw in strength. We're doing that with fighters and long-range missiles. The second is to use our available mobile units to eat away at the edges of the column, harassing their flank wherever possible."

"The cav," Edge understood. He knew now why the Bemowo Piskie Training Area was practically deserted.

"Yes," Lieutenant Parker said. "All of 1st Squadron, 2nd Cavalry's Strykers moved out yesterday. They're heading northeast, on a course paralleling the Russian column," again the tip of the crutch drew a dirty line across the map. "The plan is to swing around onto the enemy's flank and then to hit the bastards hard and fast."

"And you want us to scout the advance, sir?" Waddingham looked up. 'Outlaw Troop' were from 4th Squadron, 2nd Cavalry.

"Yes. Our Platoon from 'Outlaw Troop' has been attached to 1st Squadron for the operation. The 'War Eagles' are assembling northeast of a little village called Norwid-Slowack. There is a bridge crossing over the Sypitki River just beyond the town's outskirts. The Squadron needs to get across that bridge if they're to fall on the Russian flank. But before that, Command needs us to scout the crossing to make sure it's not defended in strength."

"Only 2nd Platoon?" Edge looked concerned. "We're supposed to scout the advance of an entire Squadron? What about the rest of 'Outlaw Troop'?"

"Can't be spared," Lieutenant Parker said flatly. "We're simply stretched too thin. Everything else in the NATO inventory is on a road headed southeast towards Warsaw. And it's just the bridge that needs scouting. We're not expecting Russian resistance that far north of Warsaw."

Edge studied the map for a long moment and then looked away into the distance, as if visualizing the route in his mind. The sun was just beginning to burn through the morning's mist, still watery and pale and lacking warmth. He sighed, resigned.

"Okay. When are we expected to meet up with 1st Squadron?"

"Later today," Parker said. "Command wants that bridge scouted tonight in preparation for a crossing at dawn tomorrow."

Edge's face became hard with fresh resolve. He looked at Vince Waddingham and then glanced at his watch. "Let the Platoon know what's happening, Sergeant. We saddle up and move out in one hour."

"Not so fast," Lieutenant Parker grimaced before Waddingham could stride away. "There's more."

"More?"

A sudden flurry of guttural shouts and crashing noise cut the discussion short. Armed infantry were pouring out of the Polish KTO Rosomaks and forming up into clumsy ragged ranks. Edge and Waddingham looked on with initial amusement and then rising consternation as the gaggle of soldiers shuffled into straight lines.

The Company of troops were kitted out in new camouflage uniforms, some wearing helmets and others wearing tan berets at jaunty angles. Their boots were shiny black, their weapons spotless. Some soldiers wore black gloves. Amidst their ranks stood a sprinkling of young women. Several of the men in the front line looked middle aged, their closely cropped hair more grey than black.

Before them strutted a short, rotund man immaculately dressed in the uniform of a Polish Army Major, wearing a black beret. He paced along the line of soldiers with his thumbs hooked inside his belt. When he reached the end of the formation, he balanced arrogantly on the balls of his feet and withered them with a malevolent glare. Someone within the ranks barked an order and the infantry snapped to attention.

The officer pirouetted on his heel and turned to face the Polish flag that fluttered over the parade ground. He sucked in his belly and thrust out his chin arrogantly. His eyes were black and suspicious beneath wild bushy brows, and his nose was a large veiny bulb that protruded over thick petulant lips. His moustache was the same wild wiry sprawl as his eyebrows.

"Who the hell…?" Edge muttered. He could hardly believe his eyes.

"You're looking at a Company of the Polish *Wojska Obrony Terytorialnej*," Lieutenant Parker said helpfully. "Better known as the WOT."

"What exactly are they?" Sergeant Waddingham asked incredulously.

"They're the nation's new Territorial Defense Force," Parker explained. "They're the brainchild of the country's former Defense Minister who decided, back in 2017, that Poland needed a fifth armed forces branch. So he created the WOT and filled its ranks with reservists and volunteers. Then he poured a huge wad of money into fancy new equipment, including a shipment of our FGM-148 Javelin anti-tank guided missiles. Finally, he padded out the troop numbers with a few army regulars. This is the result."

"Christ," Edge gasped. "Do they fight?"

"Oh, none of them have ever experienced combat," the Lieutenant went on airily. "But I imagine they will before this war is over."

"And they have Javelins?"

"One for every vehicle…"

"I've never seen them before…"

"No. They exercise on weekends on a twice-monthly basis over a period of three years. You're looking at some of the first volunteers. They've had a grand total of sixteen days basic training, and a lot of the NCO's are graduates of an express course that lasts just a couple of weeks."

Edge and Waddingham exchanged appalled looks. "The Russians are going to eat them alive," Edge offered his appraisal.

The Lieutenant grunted. Edge noticed Parker's gaze was fixed on the commanding officer.

"Do you know him?" Edge nudged.

The Lieutenant's lips curled into a derisive sneer. "I'm afraid so," he said. "That pompous little bastard is Major Andrzej Nowakowski."

"You've met him?"

Parker nodded. "Yesterday for a briefing. He thinks he's the next Napoleon."

"And he's not?"

"No, of course he bloody-well isn't," Parker's temper boiled over and, unbidden, he launched into an unfiltered tirade. "He's nothing but a trumped-up politician in a fancy uniform. Christ, Edge. That's the problem I've been trying to warn you about. The government leaders in this country believe their troops should be the first to strike a telling blow against the Russians. They say it's a matter of national pride and they're making a diplomatic issue of it. They think it will build defiance and resolve in the populace – and they refuse to allow the 1st Squadron across the bridge at Norwid-Slowack unless WOT troops are there to join in the attack on the Russian flank. That's what I've been trying to explain all along. You have to take the Polish militia with you."

*

With the support of an aide, Major Nowakowski clambered awkwardly onto the hull of the nearest KTO Rosomak and glared down at his troops, withering them with the force of his steely gaze.

"We are about to go to war!" the man clenched his fist and waved it over his head. His voice was unusually high-pitched. "Within twenty-four hours you soldiers will be the first Polish troops to face the Russian dogs in battle. Honor, pride and the future of our country will depend on your determination, your discipline and your willingness to sacrifice yourselves for the Motherland. Let none amongst you fail me, or else you will suffer the consequences."

The speech was met with stoic silence. The soldiers stared straight ahead, standing rigidly at attention while the Major's ominous threats washed over them.

With a flourish, he unholstered his sidearm and brandished the weapon. "I will shoot the first soldier who shows their back to the enemy…"

Standing beside the Stryker, Edge and Waddingham exchanged incredulous glances.

Lieutenant Parker shook his head and gave Edge a sideways peek. "The Major needs to meet you – but this doesn't seem to be an opportune moment," he understated tactfully. The Polish soldiers began forming up into their three Platoons and then marched off the parade ground towards a muddy field behind a cluster of storage sheds. "It might be a good chance to meet your new squad leader and gather the rest of the Platoon." Parker looked at his watch and made a quick calculation. "Let's say an hour to refuel and re-arm the vehicles and weapons? I'll meet you back here at 0900."

Edge and Waddingham gathered up their kit and bundled it into the Stryker. The rest of 2nd Platoon were waiting for them outside the US troop barracks. Edge filled the men in quickly on their new mission and introduced himself to the

Staff Sergeant (E-6) who would command the fourth vehicle. He was a stocky bow-legged Texan who walked like a cowboy and spoke with a John Wayne drawl. His name was Hal Calhoun. On his right sleeve he wore a combat patch displaying a pattern of four ivy leaves.

"You saw action with the 4th?"

Calhoun nodded. "I was with the Second Stryker Brigade Combat Team in Afghanistan."

Edge smiled and shook Calhoun's hand. "It's good to have another experienced man in the team. Welcome to 2nd Platoon, 'Outlaw Troop'."

"Looking forward to getting my hands dirty," the Texan drawled.

"Well you won't have long to wait," Edge confided. "We'll be back in harm's way before the end of the day. After that, well God knows what's going to happen."

At 0850 the four vehicles braked to a halt on the edge of the parade ground in a neat column. During their absence a military field tent had been erected on the grassy verge. The Americans climbed down from their Strykers, and stared agape.

"They're unbelievable," one of the Platoon's scouts croaked.

The Polish infantry were returning from drills. They marched onto the vast concrete pad, their faces smeared with mud, their uniforms grimy. Their weapons were dull and dirty. The soldiers shuffled forward in weary step, some breathless, some sagging with exhaustion. They looked nothing like the pristine Company that had first spilled so energetically out of their troop carriers less than an hour before.

Hal Calhoun shook his head in disbelief and uttered the question that everyone else in the Platoon wanted answered. "Who the hell are those guys?"

"They're the Polish *Wojska* something something," Edge said.

"The who?"

"They're a new kind of Polish militia. They're going to be travelling in convoy to the battlefront with us."

As the scouts watched on with incredulity the bedraggled soldiers shuffled into their Platoons, herded and cajoled by their NCO's. They stood at attention dripping water and mud until Major Nowakowski finally appeared from within the field tent. He strutted along the front rank of the Company and fixed each soldier with a dark-eyed, bad-tempered scowl. When he reached the far end of the line he clasped his hands behind his back and thrust out his chin.

"You are fortunate to have the opportunity to lay down your lives in defense of the Motherland, and you are lucky indeed to have me as your commander. But my vast military expertise alone will not be enough to bring valor and glory. You must fight like demons. You must show no fear. You must be disciplined and determined."

He let the final words of his battle-cry echo around the parade ground for a few menacing seconds and then abruptly dismissed the soldiers. They fell out with sighs of exhausted relief.

Lieutenant Parker dug his elbow into Edge's ribs and then propped himself upright on his crutches. "Come on," he fortified himself. "It's time to enter the dragon's lair."

Chapter 2:

Edge and Lieutenant Parker ducked under the canvas tent flap to find themselves standing at the end of a long fold-out bench. Six Polish officers, with glasses and wine bottles before them, sat on either side, with Major Nowakowski seated at the head of the table.

"Lieutenant! So glad you have arrived," the Major greeted Parker with buoyant pleasure. "I trust your ankle is not giving you too much inconvenience. Let me introduce you to my Company officers."

He made the introductions quickly. Each man nodded a somber greeting as their name was announced. They looked like dry, fussy administrators who had spent their careers behind a desk. Parker doubted any of them had fired a weapon, let alone seen combat.

"And allow me to introduce Sergeant First Class Thomas Edge," Parker shuffled aside in the cramped space.

Edge nodded his head. "Good morning, gentlemen."

Major Nowakowski studied Edge carefully, his gaze appraising. He noticed the combat patch on Edge's right sleeve but focused on the man's rumpled, sweat-stained uniform. His eyes became cunning.

"Do you always sleep in your uniform, Sergeant Edge?" the Major mocked. He flicked his gaze around the table with a thin smirk on his lips. The rest of his officers tittered in sycophantic support.

"For the last four days, Major – yes," Edge answered levelly. "It's a compromise scouts have to make whenever we are on a covert reconnaissance mission inside enemy territory."

The Major's eyes darkened and turned hostile. For another few seconds the two men studied each other and Edge's chin lifted firmly as he met and held the Polish Major's glare. Finally, Major Nowakowski swung his attention back to Lieutenant Parker. "Take a seat, Lieutenant, so we can begin the briefing. Sergeant Edge – you don't mind standing in the corner do you? We simply can't fit another chair in such a small space," the effusive politeness was brittle.

Tom Edge nodded, understanding he was caught in some undeclared clash of egos. Parker recognized the power-play as well. With the silky skill of a politician he shook his head, parrying the Major's lunge.

"Getting up and down with this damned ankle and these crutches is a bother, Major," he smiled disarmingly. "I think it's best if SFC Edge takes my seat at the table. After all, he will be the man guiding your Company forward."

Major Nowakowski gave a curt dismissive nod and turned to the officer at his right elbow. They put their heads together, and the Major spoke softly and quickly. The officer produced a map of northern Poland – much more detailed than the one Parker had shown Edge earlier. The Polish officers spread the map out and weighted the ends down with wine bottles. Major Nowakowski got to his feet, resting his clenched fists on the benchtop.

"The Russians are cunning bastards," he declared solemnly, investing his officers with the benefit of his vast military knowledge. "So we must match them with our cleverness and then defeat them with our combat skills." He traced a line with the tip of his finger showing the route to the village of Norwid-Slowack and then pressed his thumb down on the blue wiggling line of the Sypitki River. "The bridge across the river is key to our flank attack. We must seize it with speed and daring!"

Around the table, the Polish officers leaned closer and studied the terrain while the Major went on.

"We are on the verge of history, gentlemen," his voice filled with patriotic fervor. "The victory we will win once we cross the bridge and plunder the Russian column's flank will make us national heroes. But first we must reach Norwid-Slowack to join up with our American Cavalry allies, and for that menial task we will rely on the services of Sergeant Edge's Platoon of Cavalry scouts."

Heads turned. Edge nodded, but said nothing. To him, the Polish Major's speech was all just fanciful chest-beating nonsense. He glanced out through the open tent flap. The Polish militia were sitting in small groups, fastidiously cleaning their equipment. He imagined them in combat against a crack Russian infantry unit and doubted they would last more than a few seconds.

"Sergeant Edge?"

He realized with a start that his name had been called, and he turned around. Major Nowakowski had a bemused expression on his face.

"Sir?"

"I asked you, Sergeant Edge," Nowakowski said with patient restraint, "what you think of my Company?"

"Sir?" Beside him, he sensed Lieutenant Parker tense visibly and shift his weight on his crutches. Then something hard struck his ankle beneath the table as a warning.

The Major's smile became fixed, and his eyes hardened. "Well...?"

"Against experienced Russian infantry? They'll get slaughtered, Major. Within the first minute of a firefight half of them will be dead and the other half will be in full retreat," Edge spoke flatly.

For a long volcanic moment Major Nowakowski said nothing. The men around the table turned pale. Edge kept going.

"Your troops are barely trained. They have good equipment, but I doubt they even know how to use it effectively. And running around a grassy field won't help them when they get into battle. They need to know how to fight, and they need to know how to hide. Their only advantage will be surprise. In a toe-to-toe engagement, the Russians will chew them up and spit out their bones."

Major Nowakowski looked deeply offended. He leaned over the table.

"Well, well, well. Listen to the great American soldier," the Major mocked. "And just how many battles have you fought, Sergeant Edge?"

"More than I care to remember – sir," he inflected the honorific with a tinge of insolence.

"And you claim that my troops need to know how to fight and how to hide if they are to defeat the Russians?"

"Yes. Ambush is their only chance of securing an advantage."

"And you know all about ambush skills, don't you Sergeant Edge? You're one of America's highly-skilled elite Cavalry scouts. No doubt you're an expert on camouflage and ambush techniques. Isn't that so?"

Edge hesitated. He sensed he was being manipulated by the Polish Major. The man's tone had become shrewd. But he shrugged and answered honestly.

"Yes."

"Good!" Major Nowakowski slammed his hand down on the benchtop. "Then you will share your unique skills and knowledge with some of my troops."

"Sir?" Lieutenant Parker cut across the brittle silence, his voice mortified. "There is no time for our scouts to coach your Company on the art of camouflage and ambush. The commander of 1st Cav Squadron is awaiting your arrival northeast of Norwid-Slowack. If we're going to seize the bridge over the Sypitki your infantry must move out now." Which wasn't technically true, everyone in the tent knew. It was fifty miles to Norwid-Slowack. Even allowing for a circuitous cross-country route, the journey would take just a few hours.

"No!" the Major shook his head. "Until Sergeant Edge teaches at least two of my soldiers the skills of camouflage, we will not move out, and your army will not seize the bridge. My answer is final."

Parker shot Edge a withering glare, his eyes hectic with flustered alarm. "Give me a moment, Major. I need to talk to Sergeant Edge – alone."

Parker hobbled out into the daylight. Edge followed. Parker wheeled around, his face livid with outrage.

"Have you gone completely fucking mad?" the Lieutenant exploded in rare anger.

Edge said nothing.

Parker's lips twitched and there was a froth of tiny bubbles at the corner of his mouth. He scraped his hand through his hair and then poked Edge in the chest. "Go back in there and apologize. Tell the Major you're an ignorant ass. Tell him you were concussed. Tell him anything you bloody-well like, but make sure whatever you say includes the words 'I'm very sorry', understand?"

"No," Edge said. "I won't apologize."

"Christ!" Parker exploded. He tried to appeal to Edge's sense of logic. "Fuck your pride, Sergeant. An entire counter attack… an opportunity to swing onto the flank of the invading Russians hangs in the balance. A delay of even a day might cost us the chance to strike. There is more at stake than your fucking feelings."

"I didn't start this, Lieutenant. The Major did. All I can be accused of is telling the truth."

"The truth?" Parker looked at Edge like the man was insane. "What has the truth got to do with it? This is politics you crazy bastard. Politics!"

"Yes, sir."

Parker was not convinced by Edge's sudden capitulation. "Don't make me order you…" his voice dropped and became scathingly quiet.

"I want two hours."

"What?"

"I want two hours," Edge said with determination. "If I can't teach a couple of the Polish soldiers the basics of camouflage by 1100 hours, I will apologize to the Major."

Parker saw the stubborn resolve in Edge's eyes. He glanced at his watch and stiffened.

"Sergeant Edge, you and I never had this conversation. Do you understand?" Lieutenant Parker said formally.

"Yes, sir."

"In fifteen minutes, I am boarding a helicopter to Warsaw and then flying back to the States. I have been in my quarters for the past thirty minutes packing. I saw you for the last time this morning when I briefed you on the mission and then advised you to meet with Major Nowakowski. I have not seen you since."

"Yes, sir." The two men saluted and Edge wondered if he saw a trace of wicked amusement in the Lieutenant's eyes before he disappeared towards the barracks building, crabbing awkwardly on his crutches.

Edge stepped back inside the tent. Major Nowakowski still stood, leaning over the bench.

"Two of your people, and I want two hours," Edge said.

"Agreed," the Major's smile was thin with triumph. He glanced at his watch. "You have until 1100 hours to teach effective camouflage skills to two of my soldiers. If you can conceal their location from me, we will move with all haste towards Norwid-Slowack where your 1st Cavalry Squadron awaits our arrival. But if you fail, Sergeant Edge," the Polish Major's voice betrayed a gleeful anticipation, "you will issue a public apology, on the parade ground, to my entire Company."

*

The two Polish militia reported to a leafy grove of scrubland where NATO troops practiced small arms exercises. Edge and Waddingham were waiting for them in the Stryker beneath a tree on the fringe of the clearing. One of the base Humvees was parked alongside.

The man's name was Szymon. He was aged in his thirties. He had a voice as soft as a girl and an effeminate face, with big toffee-colored eyes behind steel-rimmed spectacles. He was slim and narrow-shouldered. He looked like a clerk.

The woman was named Kalina. She had a broad brow, a proud nose and a wide mouth. Her expression was serious, her features classically Slavic. She had dark boldly-arched eyebrows and her hair was drawn back severely from her face and tucked in a bun beneath her helmet. She was younger than the man; Edge guessed her to be in her mid-twenties. They squatted down in the grass beside the Stryker. Vince Waddingham appeared from inside the vehicle carrying what looked like two bulky coats made of straw. He laid them down on the ground.

"A day from now – if the planned attack on the Russians happens – both of you are going to be dead," Edge began. "It won't be your fault. It will be because you didn't know better, and because you weren't trained properly. All I can do is teach you the basics of camouflage and concealment, so pay attention. What you're about to learn might save your lives, and it might give you the one thing you'll need to live through a firefight; the advantage of surprise."

He paused for a beat to let the magnitude of his warning sink in, then picked up a small olive-green cosmetics-like container that fitted into the palm of his hand. "This is camouflage skin paint. It's like make-up for warriors." He flipped open the box to reveal trays of colored cream in subdued natural tones and a small acrylic mirror set into the lid. "We use this to camouflage our faces, starting with the darkest color to paint the areas of your face that protrude the most." He dipped his finger into the shade of loam brown then reached out and smeared a line down the length of the Polish man's nose. Then he quickly painted the brow line, the cheeks and the thrust of his chin.

"Now the mid-tone." He dipped his finger back into the paint and smeared color over the young woman's left eye socket and across her right cheek, then kept working in lighter shades back and forth. "This is not a beauty contest," Edge warned. "We're not looking for perfection – we're looking for realistic shades of light and dark that could be found in nature. The ultimate goal is to flatten your face and disguise its human form. That's why we paint the protruding areas with the darkest colors."

He showed them the results of his work in the small mirror and handed over the compact. "Normally we work with a buddy, and the whole process should take just a few minutes. You guys can work together to finish what I started – and remember to also paint your neck, ears and hands."

Edge left the two Polish soldiers and went striding away into the grove of long grass and shrubs with Vince Waddingham at his side. The two scouts came back a few minutes later, their arms filled with twigs, leaves, tufts of long stringy grass and a handful of mud. Edge inspected the two soldiers and grunted, satisfied.

He picked up one of the straw-covered coats and showed it to the militia. "This is the jacket of a ghillie suit," he said, turning it around in his hands. "There are pants as well. The purpose of the suit is to conceal the outline of your body and to help you blend into the local environment. This one," he started pulling out the straw which was held in place by elastic straps and a layer of gauze, "was created for a covert mission in an area of dry grass. It will not help you today because the natural terrain here is different. The ghillie suit must be adapted to your environment, so each time you go on a mission you need to gather fresh camouflage from the immediate area you will be working in," he pointed at the weeds, leaves and twigs bundled at their feet. He dropped to his knees beside the Polish soldiers and began replacing the suit's straw camouflage with some of the ground debris, working quickly until the coloring better reflected the foliage around them. Then he smeared sections of the sleeves with daubed mud. He shrugged the coat on. "Combined with the pants, a suit like this is your best chance to avoid detection," Edge said. He handed the jacket to the young woman. "Now it's your turn."

The two militia worked studiously for ten minutes, bowed over the coats, their camouflaged faces frowned with concentration. Edge stood aside and watched. Waddingham came back to the Stryker carrying leafy twigs and more mud.

When the task was finished, the soldiers stripped off their uniforms and slipped into the ghillie suits. Edge and Waddingham fussed over them like a mother making final adjustments to her teenage daughter's prom dress. They added extra twigs and leaves until experience told them the camouflage was complete. The outfits were topped off with floppy-brimmed hats, covered by a ragged veil of camouflage net.

Edge and Waddingham exchanged glances. Waddingham winked. "I've seen worse."

The final step was to camouflage the weapons. The Polish were armed with the new MSBS/GROT assault rifle. Edge showed the militia how to disguise the lines of the barrel with strips of burlap and smears of camouflage paint.

Waddingham nudged Edge and showed the face of his watch. Time was almost up. Edge grimaced. There had been no opportunity to teach the recruits how to crawl with stealth, nor how to trail their spare equipment behind them in a drag bag.

Edge drove back to the parade ground to collect Major Nowakowski in the Humvee, and Vince Waddingham drew the two Polish militia aside for a final instructional talk.

"The secret of concealment is to find the right firing position. You do that by studying the ground," Waddingham explained. "Look for areas with the most foliage and the most trap shadow. Look for locations that have a front drop of cover and a back drop of higher bushes. If you can find a firing position in that channel of light and shade, you will be between cover to your front and rear. That makes you damned hard to spot from fifty yards – provided you stay still and don't do anything stupid."

The Polish soldiers nodded, attentive and grim. Waddingham glanced towards the parade ground. There was still no sign of the returning Humvee, but he knew it would only be a matter of moments before the vehicle appeared.

"You have ten minutes to go and find yourself a firing position," he said. "Sergeant Edge will bring your Major to the tree where the Stryker is parked. Don't fuck this up. What happens next is up to you."

*

The Humvee appeared a few minutes later and braked to a halt beneath the tree. Major Nowakowski clambered down from the vehicle and took a moment to vainly straighten his uniform and adjust the angle of his beret. He had a confident, cocky smile on his face. With him was a uniformed aide. The man fetched a fold out camp chair from the vehicle and set it down beside a fringe of green bushes.

"So, Sergeant Edge, tell me how your instruction went."

"Fine, Major," Edge said. "The soldiers you sent were good students."

"Good enough to conceal themselves from the enemy?"

"I think so."

Major Nowakowski smiled thinly. He had a pair of binoculars hanging from a strap around his neck. "But not good enough to hide from my experienced eye. I am no Russian recruit, Sergeant Edge. I have been too long in the military to be fooled by casual camouflage."

"You have five minutes, Major," Edge declared. "That's more time than any Russian spotter would have."

The grove was on the fringe of a wooded stand, threaded with walking trails where exercising NATO troops practiced patrol skills. The area opened up onto a broad field of vehicle and mortar-churned ground, sprinkled with low shrubby bushes and stunted trees. The grass between the pockets of cover was long and lush, waving gently in the breeze.

"Agreed," Major Nowakowski glanced at his watch. He looked over his shoulder and barked at the aide who carried two-way radios in his hand. "Cybulski, get out into the field, man, and listen for my directions. I'll steer you right on top of them."

With the Major calling instructions, the hapless aide was made to bound through the field of grass like a hunting dog, jinking left and right to each fresh instruction.

"No, you damned fool!" Major Nowakowski berated. "I said *left*!"

The minutes ticked by. Edge kept an eye on his watch, counting down the seconds. Vince Waddingham sidled up beside him. "How much longer?"

"Another minute," Edge muttered.

Sensing the deadline approaching, Major Nowakowski leaped to his feet with the binoculars pressed hard to his eyes. The two-way was in his free hand as he guided the aide towards a suspicious clump of leafy ground a hundred yards directly ahead.

"More to your right… more… now left, Cybulski. There! *Right there!*"

The aide crouched down then rose slowly back to his feet. He shook his head.

"Damn!" the Major growled.

"Time!" Edge had counted down the last few seconds holding his breath. He let out a sigh of relief then cupped his hands to his mouth. "Okay, Szymon, you are clear to reveal yourself."

A few seconds later the Polish man stood up. He emerged like an apparition from a patch of non-descript grass to the right, just seventy yards away. Major Nowakowski blinked in shock. The aide had never come within twenty yards of the firing spot. Even Edge was impressed.

"Come out, Kalina!" Edge called again. He let his gaze sweep the open field, expecting to see the young woman reveal herself.

A sudden squeal of fright broke the silence. Major Nowakowski's eyes were wide with fear, his face frozen, mouth agape. He was making a pitiful mewling sound – because there was a hand wrapped around his ankle.

A woman's hand.

The Polish girl had concealed herself in the bushy shrub right beside the Major's chair, not five feet away from where he had stood.

"*Gówno!*" the Major swore vehemently. He kicked his leg free of the woman's clutches and flushed with anger and humiliation. Then he rounded on Edge and his eyes were terrible, his voice shaking with rage. "You are too clever, Sergeant Edge. Too clever for your own good." The Major's tone dripped menace and foreboding. He looked like he had more to say but instead he bit his tongue and stormed off, barking for the aide to follow him.

Edge checked his watch. "My Platoon of Cavalry scouts are leaving this training area in thirty minutes, Major. If you want us to screen your column's advance north to the 1st Squadron, I suggest you make immediate preparations to move out."

*

The four Strykers of 2nd Platoon, 'Outlaw Troop' moved out in a staggered column formation, the vehicles dispersed as protection against any threat of a possible Russian air attack. Edge stood in his command hatch in front of Vince Waddingham who was pulling rear air guard in the open hatch behind him. Their headsets were plugged into the vehicle's internal comms.

Both men's expressions were hidden behind the dark lenses of their Revision goggles – but Waddingham didn't need to see his Platoon Sergeant's eyes to know what he was thinking.

He had seen Edge this way before; deep in pensive contemplation after a mission, when he would withdraw from everyone around him to reflect on the events, and to ask himself whether he had handled the conflict to the best of his ability.

The brooding could make Edge a morose, miserable bastard sometimes, Waddingham acknowledged – but he supposed it was what also made him a good leader of men.

Though why he was dwelling on the sharp exchange of words with the Polish Major had Waddingham dumbfounded.

He wondered then if maybe Edge was still fretting over the outbreak of war, and his home life. Waddingham simply could not understand why any man would want to marry and start a family. For him life was much simpler; women were plentiful, and every day was an adventure meant to be experienced – and you couldn't do that tied down by domesticity. Waddingham liked to live dangerously… because there wasn't any other way to *really* live. He was a free spirit, without a care in the world.

"Wanna talk about it?" he leaned across the Stryker's gunners mount and spoke above the relentless revving noises of the vehicle's engine and the wind in their faces.

"What?"

"Whatever's on your mind."

Edge said nothing. He swung his head round and watched the rest of the Platoon's vehicles coming on behind them. Closer to the horizon he could see the billowing dust cloud thrown up by the Polish KTO Rosomaks trailing in their wake.

"Are you worried about the Polish Major?"

"None of your concern, Sergeant," Edge said harshly.

"Okay," Waddingham nodded without any intention of relenting. The two men were friends; a bond formed in combat during the Afghanistan campaign, and the relationships formed during battle were more enduring than those between casual acquaintances. They had seen each other scared, seen each other on the point of despair. They had shared hardships and the frustration of countless 'hurry up and wait' situations.

"Major Nowakowski is a pimped-up fuckin' peacock if you ask me," Waddingham offered his opinion blithely.

"I didn't," Edge became surly.

"Didn't what?"

"I didn't bloody ask you."

Yet despite himself, Edge felt his silent concerns bubbling to the surface. He understood what Vince Waddingham was doing – encouraging him to speak his mind – and in a way he appreciated it. Suddenly everything weighing on him spilled out in a rush.

"Nowakowski might be a useless peacock, but he's got influence," Edge said. "The Lieutenant told me he was some kind of politician. So he can make things difficult. And on top of that I don't know how much pull he's going to have with the Lieutenant Colonel," Edge frowned and then admonished himself. "I should have just shut my fucking mouth. I had nothing to prove. I could have just walked away from his challenge and left his dignity intact. In twenty-four hours he would have been out of our lives."

Waddingham shrugged. "He still will be. Once we get across this bridge…"

"Maybe," Edge sounded fatalistic and gloomy. "But how hard is the next day going to be, and how much harder is that bastard going to make it for us now I've embarrassed him?"

Chapter 3:

The Strykers of 1st Squadron were concealed in a vast stretch of dense woodland eight miles to the west of Norwid-Slowack. Edge's Platoon arrived in the middle of the afternoon. As Edge's vehicle swerved off the road and nosed into the dappled shadows of the forest, he noticed two camouflaged Stryker A1 IM-SHORAD's on air defense duty. The vehicles were new, armed with Hellfire and Stinger missiles.

Deeper into the woods Edge discovered the TOC, surrounded by two M1130 Command Strykers and a scatter of Humvees. The tents of the Tactical Operations Center had been set up in a clearing of mossy, muddy ground overhung by tall trees. The scouts dismounted their vehicles and stretched weary muscles. The lead KTO Rosomak appeared a few minutes later and slewed to an abrupt halt, spattering mud and digging deep tire trenches in the soft earth. Behind the first Wolverine, the rest of the Polish vehicles parked in a chaotic litter between the trees. The troops dismounted from their vehicles, irritable, hungry and tired.

Major Nowakowski stepped down from the lead vehicle like an actor making a grand entrance. He tightened his lips and gave Edge an unfriendly glance.

An aide appeared from the nearest tent. He wore the harried frown of a low-level functionary. He feigned a smile and threw the Polish Major a salute.

"Welcome, Major Nowakowski," the aide said with effusive politeness. "Everyone is inside waiting for you," he glanced sideways to let Edge know that he was not included. "Please follow me."

Edge watched the Polish Major disappear inside the TOC and turned his attention to his men and their machines. Twenty minutes later he received an abrupt summons.

The TOC tent was twenty feet long, supported by three steel collapsible 'Y' frames from which were hung fluorescent lights. The floor was covered in rubber matting and the interior filled with folding tables and chairs. Most of the chairs were occupied by staff and much of the table surface littered with communication equipment, cables, water bottles, discarded helmets and intelligence imagery.

Lieutenant Colonel Marion Sutcliffe, commander of the 'War Eagles' 1st Cavalry Squadron was a tall, thin-faced man with deep-set intelligent eyes surrounded by a fine web of wrinkles. He had the sun-browned features of a man who was accustomed to staring at far horizons. He moved with energy and urgency, extending his hand as the aide led Edge into the tent's darkened gloom.

"Sergeant Edge. I hope your troopers are ready to work."

Edge nodded.

Another man stepped forward. He introduced himself as a NATO Brigade Liaison Officer. He wore a uniform Edge had never seen before and wore it awkwardly. He looked, Edge guessed, more like a Brussels diplomat than a soldier. He had a dry, desiccated voice, thin fussy hands and smelled faintly of cologne. His manner was impatient and brusque.

Edge sat at the far end of the table. He sensed underlying tension as though he had been brought to the briefing in the midst of an argument. The Lieutenant Colonel and his staff were grim-faced and tight lipped. Major Nowakowski sat with his arms folded stubbornly and a flush of temper on his cheeks.

"Now everyone is assembled and in agreement," the NATO Officer said with significance in a thick German accent, "perhaps we can discuss the details of the mission."

The Squadron's S-2 and S-3 brought the meeting up to date with the progress of the Russian column heading towards Warsaw and then sharpened their focus to the area surrounding the village of Norwid-Slowack. The available satellite imagery was old; US spy services were overburdened with tasks across the length and breadth of Europe so there had been no updated images for the past eighteen hours.

Edge was handed one of the photographs and he studied it for a long moment. The grainy image showed the erratic line of the Sypitki River and in the bottom left corner the village of Norwid-Slowack. The settlement was an untidy sprawl of around fifty buildings built on either side of a road that crossed the river and continued north through the saddle of a long ridge. Smaller knolls of high ground hunched close to the riverbank on both sides. A second image showed an enlargement of the bridge itself between a fringe of riverbank bushes.

Marion Sutcliffe took over the briefing, addressing Edge directly. His tone was strained with bitterness as though he approached a delicate point that had been argued before Edge arrived.

"Sergeant, your mission is to take a dismounted patrol forward under the cover of darkness to scout the approach to the bridge northeast of the village. We want you to discover whether it is defended by the enemy and if so, at what strength. Our crossing is planned for sunrise tomorrow morning. The attack will be led by Major Nowakowski's armored vehicles and his Territorial Defense Force Company." It sounded as though it aggrieved the Cavalry commander to utter the words, and Edge suspected this point was the source of the awkwardness he sensed. "The Polish column will be supported by mortars on the outskirts of the village and our Strykers close behind them."

"But my troops will be first across the bridge. I insist on this fact," Major Nowakowski did not address Lieutenant Colonel Sutcliffe but instead turned to the NATO Officer, waving his finger. "Unless this is clearly agreed, there will be no crossing. None!"

"We have already arbitrated the point, Major," the NATO officer confirmed with a tired sigh. "Is there anything else to be discussed?"

The men around the tent curtly shook their heads. Sutcliffe gave Edge a sideways glance. The Lieutenant Colonel looked eager for the briefing to end. "You'll get your formal OPORD later today, Sergeant," Sutcliffe said. OPORDS were a formal five paragraph set of instructions for a mission that included details of the situation, the objective of the mission, the method of execution, the administration and the command signals. "In the meantime, I suggest you and your men get some chow and some rest. I have a feeling it's going to be a long, uncomfortable night…"

*

It was 0100 hours when the Stryker braked to a halt behind one of several low knolls that stood to the east of Norwid-Slowack. Edge climbed to the top of the rise with Waddingham and two other team scouts. The four men lay amongst rocks and dirt and peered out into the night.

To their west the tiny village was cast in pale moonlight. The town's church stood at the far end of the settlement, its ancient stone bell tower clearly visible against a backdrop of stars. The village seemed deserted, or asleep.

Edge traversed his thermal binoculars towards the river, picking up the fringe of shrubs that lined the Sypitki, and then finally the outline of the bridge itself. He kept swinging the binoculars until he was looking due north, inspecting the ground between his position and the riverbank. He traced a line across the grassy meadow before them and picked out the shadowed hint of several clumped bushes.

Further east, he saw a jumble of broken ground and the skeletal remains of a building. It might once have been a barn, or perhaps a small farm shed. Now only ruins remained. It was a tempting place for concealment, but Edge guessed the distance to the bridge to be almost a hundred yards. There were a number of bushes closer, although they afforded less cover. One in particular caught his eye. It was a clump of wild shrubs about thirty yards short of the bridge and about the same distance from the verge of the road. He steered Waddingham's gaze onto the site.

"There," he said. "That's our LUP. An hour before sunrise, I'll go forward and reconnoiter the approach to the bridge."

Waddingham nodded. The four men slid back off the skyline until they were in dead ground. Edge got quickly to his feet.

"We will take the bushes," he told Waddingham then turned to the other two team scouts. "You guys will get to the ruined building and find good cover."

They marked their objectives with the vehicle commander and then prepared themselves to go forward. Edge found Waddingham with his face painted and his drag bag at his feet, suspended at the end of a long tether. "You ready?"

"Let's do it."

Edge checked his watch. It was four hours until sunrise. He estimated they would need to cross three hundred yards of grassy ground to reach the LUP.

Edge and Waddingham crept around the foot of the knoll, keeping to the patches of soft shadow until they reached a rusted fence. They dropped to their stomachs beneath a buckled line of barbed wire and began the slow crawl towards their objective. Halfway across the field they were sweating from the exertion and strain, grunting softly from the effort of dragging their bodies and equipment with painstaking stealth across the field. Edge stopped for a moment and slowly lifted his head to orientate himself. Far in the distance the long crest beyond the river was a solid black silhouette, its jagged ridgeline shown in stark relief against the lowering moon. Edge put his head back down and crawled on. His knees and elbows ached, the skin rubbed tender by relentless abrasion.

At last, and with a silent sigh of relief, the ground opened up before him and he slithered down into a waist-high depression, veiled from sight by shrubs. Edge rolled onto his back, breathing deeply, and stared up at the fading night stars. Sweat ran in runnels across his brow and dripped off his chin.

Vince Waddingham appeared on the lip of the depression several minutes later. Edge pulled him down into cover and the two men sat hunched close together until their heartbeats steadied and their breathing became regular.

Edge checked his watch. There were ninety-five minutes until sunrise.

The two men rolled onto their stomachs and crawled silently forward to the lip of the depression. Through the screen of bushes to their front they could hear the soft burble of the river nearby. Edge took the thermal binoculars from his drag bag and studied the bridge.

Then, suddenly, a hoarse voice whispered Edge's name from out of the darkness. He spun his head, a lump of alarm rising thick in his throat. The grass close to the depression swayed unnaturally in the still night. The voice called again, strained but still a whisper.

A figure emerged out of the darkness, crawling awkwardly. The shadowy shape dropped down into the depression in a small puff of dust and a tumble of limbs. Edge pounced on the man, going for his weapon. He heard a sharp intake of painful breath and then a paint-streaked face loomed out of the moonlit darkness.

With a shock, Edge recognized the Polish woman he had trained at Bemowo Piskie. He seized her wrist in a vice-like grip and pinned her down to the ground.

"Kalina? What the fuck are you doing?" Edge hissed. Their faces were just inches apart, his voice hoarse.

"I have orders," she winced. Edge was lying on top of her, crushing the air from her lungs.

"I could have fucking shot you. Jesus!"

"I have orders," the young woman whispered again. "Direct from Major Nowakowski. He told me to deliver them personally."

"How did you find us?"

"Your vehicle commander showed me the position you had selected."

Edge and Waddingham exchanged glances. In the darkness Waddingham's features were a camouflaged blur, but Edge sensed the other man's suspicion.

Edge rolled off the woman. She lay for a moment, breathing hoarsely, her knees drawn up to her chest. Waddingham leaned across the ditch and whispered to Edge, "I don't like this, man."

"Neither do I," Edge said.

He eyed the young woman carefully, his lips pressed into a grim line of foreboding. "What are the new orders?"

"General Nowakowski wants you to reconnoiter the far side of the bridge – not just the approach," she said softly. "He said that because Polish troops will be making the first crossing; it is important to know if the bridge is wired with explosives, or if the far ridge is defended with Russian tanks."

Edge sat back on his heels and stared blankly into the distance. It was a suicide mission. It was vengeance for humiliating the Polish Major.

Vince Waddingham reached into his drag bag for the radio. "Fuck that," he hissed vehemently. "Let's see what the Lieutenant Colonel has to say."

"No," Edge said, stilling Waddingham's hand. But then a wave of bitter resentment overwhelmed him.

"Bastard! What a vile, petty, pox-faced, vengeful fucking prima Dona. What a fucking cowardly, incompetent cretin." He bunched his fist and punched at the dirt in a fit of impotent frustration. Then he wheeled on the woman, his jaw clenched and his eyes savage.

"Fine. Go back and tell that arrogant primped up peacock I'll reconnoiter the far side of the bridge."

"No," Kalina shook her head sadly. "I won't go back. And I won't call him those names."

"You have orders to stay with us?"

"Yes," she said. "But also, Major Nowakowski is my father."

*

The three figures lay in the dirt, side-by-side, their faces powdered in a thin film of dust. The night was eerily silent.

Low in the starlit sky the moon began to fade, presaging the coming dawn.

Edge lifted his head above the rim of the depression and peered through the screen of foliage, his gaze picking up the bank of the Sypitki River and the silhouette of the steel-trussed bridge. Further into the distance, the ridge on the far side of the river loomed as a black brooding menace.

Edge sank back down out of sight and glanced at his watch. "Five more minutes," he muttered.

Neither Waddingham or Kalina replied. They were pre-occupied; caught up in the snare of their own rising anxieties. At sunrise the Polish militia and the entire 1st Squadron, 2nd Cavalry would appear behind them, the column of armored troop carriers snaking down the narrow road, through the village and out onto the open plain. If the bridge was heavily defended by Russians, the chances the Cavalry could make a successful crossing would be dramatically reduced. Just two T-90 tanks, hull-down and supported by heavy machine guns, could turn the road into a charnel house of slaughter.

Edge checked his watch again. He could feel the flutter of anxiety in his guts; the nervous apprehension that made his hands tremble and turned his mouth dry.

"Fuck it," he growled. "I'm going now."

Vince Waddingham said nothing. He shifted position until he was laying with the barrel of his M4 resting on the rim of the depression to offer covering fire. Kalina rolled six feet to her left, her sudden movement kicking up a little cloud of dirt. She came up into a kneeling position and sighted her weapon on the steel frame of the bridge, left elbow braced on her left knee, the butt of her automatic weapon pulled tight against her shoulder. She gave Edge a short nodding jerk of her head.

Edge scrambled over the lip of the depression and rose to a cautious crouch. After laying prone throughout the interminable wait his legs felt rubbery beneath him. He could feel his heart pound against the cage of his ribs. He waited for the wicked retort of an enemy rifle, his whole body tensed for the hammer-blow impact.

Nothing.

Edge took a dozen cautious steps forward, weapon raised, finger curled around the trigger, his eyes wide, his head turning ceaselessly. He stopped suddenly and froze, his senses alert and his head cocked to the side. He stood like that – unmoving and tensed – for a full thirty seconds while rivulets of sweat trickled down his back.

When he finally reached the shadows of the bridge, he was trembling with pent-up tension. He threw himself down into the long grass. He could hear his own breath sawing loudly in his ears. He scanned the far bank of the river, fringed by a low hedge of bushes, and remained motionless for long minutes. In the fading moonlight, the surface of the Sypitki looked like a ribbon of soft grey silk.

He got to his feet and leaned against a steel girder of the bridge. The metal was cold, the grey paint flaking to reveal rusted rivets. Standing in the soft light, he felt exposed and vulnerable.

With a tremendous effort of will, he pushed himself upright and stepped onto the open roadway. The gravel crunched beneath his feet; the sound so loud it made him cringe. Before him the steel truss bridge across the Sypitki was two lanes wide, the bridge deck covered in asphalt, the guardrail bowed and buckled in several places. The steel support beams were painted grey, streaked with years of rust. The abutments along the shoreline were concrete slabs surrounded by boulders that were dark with green slime and smeared with muddy tidelines.

With sweat trickling into his eyes, Edge took a step forward and then another, pacing cautiously, keeping close to the guardrail. He breathed through his open mouth. His legs felt stiff and jerking, his heart hammered.

He reached the far side of the bridge and stepped down onto the sloping approach slab. The shoulder of the road was gravel-covered, falling away to a fringe of dense bush. Edge took three more paces and stopped abruptly. The road before him curved to the left and then passed between the saddle of two long tree-covered ridges. Edge scanned the darkened rise, looking for tell-tale signs that the crossing was defended. Around him the horizon became lit with the first watery glow of the approaching dawn.

A sudden small movement caught Edge's eye. He turned his head casually towards the lower slopes of the nearest ridge and was about to dismiss it as a rustle of leaves. But the pre-dawn was still and airless...

The movement came again; so slight that this time he sensed it more than saw it, and the first chill draught of apprehension blew down his spine.

Edge looked away, feigning casual indifference, and dropped to one knee to scoop up a fistful of gravel. He let the dirt trickle through his clenched hand and trained his eyes back to the spot without moving his head. In the periphery of his vision, he saw the outline of a man's helmet covered in camouflage net. For long seconds he was stunned, frozen by the shock of it. His senses strained tight with a sudden fizz of adrenaline.

Now Edge saw the whole picture. A man lay crouched behind a fallen tree trunk. He was wearing a camouflage smock and cradling an automatic weapon to his shoulder. Beside the man was concealed another soldier, lying prone amidst a thicket of leaves and ground cover. It was a machine gun post, situated to enfilade the bridge. Then the outline of a third soldier materialized to the left of the others, his body half-hidden behind a boulder.

Edge turned away from the ridge and rose slowly to his feet. He started to walk back across the bridge taking slow measured steps.

He flexed his arms and felt the space between his shoulder blades and imagined the devastating impact of a bullet as it tore into his back and exploded out through his chest. His skin prickled from the flesh-crawling stings of his fear.

Edge reached the middle of the bridge. The dawn's light came on quickly, pushing back the veil of night to reveal the new day. The upper works of the bridge's steel frame took form, and the rooftops of the distant village buildings had shape. A flock of waterfowl splashed across the river's glassy surface and then took to noisy flight.

Go!

Edge started to run.

He broke into a desperate sprint, his arms pumping, his head thrown back. He had the terrifying sensation of time slowing, so that the dash to the end of the bridge seemed to take forever, his boots dragging leadenly in the gravel.

The sudden wicked sound of a single shot split the still morning; a high-pitched *'thwack'* that echoed across the plain. The bullet ricocheted off an iron bridge truss, the projectile passing so close to Edge that he felt the heat of it like a hot breath against his cheek. He jinked left, then right. His knees buckled. He reached the verge of the road and flung himself down the slope. A second bullet kicked up an eruption of dirt by his boots. Then he was in the long grass, tucked into a tight ball and rolling, tumbling. He bounced to his feet and sprinted for the depression. He saw Waddingham and Kalina hunched over their weapons. He swerved left to clear their field of fire, lifting his knees high, his face wrenched in desperate effort.

Vince Waddingham sprayed a short burst of gunfire at the far ridge. Then Edge loomed over the crest of the hollow, his mouth hanging open, his whole body strained with exertion.

He flung himself into a desperate dive, and crashed down into cover.

*

Edge hit the ground in an awkward tumble of arms and legs. His knee cracked against his jaw and his mouth filled with blood. He was drenched in a lather of sweat. His mouth felt thick, his tongue swollen. He blinked his eyes and the pale dawn seemed as bright and blinding as an arc light. He rolled onto his side and hawked a thick gob of phlegm and blood into the dirt.

Edge groaned, then forced himself into a sitting position and scraped the back of his hand across his mouth, leaving a smear of blood across his cheek.

Dawn's light had begun to spread across the plain, catching the upper works of the bridge and the fringe of shrubs that grew along both banks of the Sypitki. The distant ridgeline seemed somehow less hostile in the soft morning light, its tree covered crest blurred behind a thin veil of mist that twisted across the surface of the river.

"What did you see?" Waddingham spoke from the rim of the depression without turning his head. His voice was urgent with anxiety.

"A machine gun post," Edge answered.

"Fuck!" Waddingham spat. "Anything else? Any armor or artillery?"

"Not that I saw – but that doesn't mean they're not there, or somewhere nearby."

"Fuck."

"Are we safe here?" Kalina interrupted.

"For now," Edge considered the question. "The Russians won't want to reveal their strength just to kill a few scouts."

"You sure about that?"

"Yeah," Edge put certainty into his voice. "But I've got a bad feeling about the crossing…" He reached into Waddingham's drag bag for the radio and a pair of binoculars, and crawled to the rim of the depression. He ran his eyes along the ridgeline. In the morning light the heights looked peaceful and tranquil. Through the high-powered glasses he quartered the ground beyond the bridge's geometric frame, studying the tree-shadowed undergrowth. He saw nothing. He picked up the Harris AN/PRC-152 radio – a handheld secure comms unit – and called 1st Squadron headquarters.

"Checkmate Six Romeo, this is Bad Karma Xray. SALUTE report, over."

"Bad Karma Xray, this is Checkmate Six Romeo prepared to copy. Send it."

"Infantry fire, defensive positions, ridge Alpha-Four-Nine, zero-five-forty-five hours, machine guns and light weapons. How copy, over?"

"Bad Karma Xray this is Checkmate Six Romeo. Good copy. Out."

Edge slid back down into the meager shelter of the depression and rolled onto his back. The sun broke through a thin veil of cloud.

*

Pacing the floor of the TOC like a caged lion, Lieutenant Colonel Sutcliffe snatched the report from his radio operator and read quickly. The 1st Squadron's Strykers were formed up on the road to Norwid-Slowack, ready to move out. Half a mile ahead of them the twelve Polish KTO Rosomak Wolverines sat with their engines idling clouds of grey exhaust into the morning air. The Polish troops were standing in tight knots around their vehicles, smoking cigarettes and drinking coffee from tin mugs.

Sutcliffe stood with his fists balled on his hips, aware that every wasted moment mattered. Beside him, Major Nowakowski lurked, stiff as a statue, his brow furrowed. Sutcliffe glanced at a map spread across the table and growled.

"Find out how much fire the scouts are taking," he demanded.

The radio operator hunched back over his equipment. "Bad Karma Xray, this is Checkmate Six Romeo. Over."

Edge snatched the radio out of the dirt. "Checkmate Six Romeo, this is Bad Karma Xray. Go."

But before the operator could ask his question, Sutcliffe leaned impulsively across the table and snatched the radio away. "Bad Karma Xray, this is Checkmate Six Actual. Report your current situation."

"Checkmate Six Actual we are thirty yards northeast of the bridge, over."

"Have you taken enemy fire, Bad Karma Xray?"

"Sniper fire only, Checkmate Six Actual, but the enemy has at least one machine gun post in position to cover the crossing…"

"Only sniper fire?"

"Confirm."

"Hold your position, Bad Karma Xray. We're advancing to the bridge." Sutcliffe broke the connection and glanced at the Polish Major, his decision made. "Get your troops mounted up. The mission is a go!"

Major Nowakowski hurried out of the TOC shouting orders.

The Lieutenant Colonel drew his Troop leaders around him. "Get your men mounted up. Our scouts report nothing but sniper fire, but I want those mortars set up on the outskirts of the village just like we planned," he singled out a Lieutenant in command of four M1129 Mortar Carriers attached to the Squadron from HHT. Then he turned his focus onto the rest of his officers. "Once the mortars are in place to cover our advance, we'll go for the bridge hard and fast. I want to be right behind the Polish column, and I want our lead elements ready to take over the attack at the first sign of trouble."

The Squadron's Troop commanders nodded gravely.

Sutcliffe issued a final reminder. "Gentlemen, the Russian spearhead is closing on Warsaw and every moment we're delayed is another mile they plunge deeper into Poland. Our mission is to attack their flank and harass their advance. This isn't the time for caution."

Chapter 4:

The attack on the bridge began as a ground tremor. Edge felt the faint vibration through his chest and he rose cautiously to his knees and looked back towards the village with the binoculars pressed to his eyes.

Four M1129 Mortar Carriers appeared in the distance. They emerged from behind a bend in the road and grew in size and detail with every passing moment until Edge could clearly see each vehicle commander standing upright in their hatches, and hear the rumble of each Stryker's engine.

The Mortar Carriers kept coming on, racing along the road, inexplicably bypassing the turnoff to the village and instead making straight towards the bridge. Edge frowned with a twinge of unease.

And still the four Strykers came on, the sound of their charge rising like a steady rumble of thunder against the tranquil peace of the new day.

"They're too close!" Edge said aloud. "They're supposed to set up firing positions on the outskirts of the village!"

"Where are they going?" Vince Waddingham also realized the imminent danger. "They're in range of machine gun fire."

Then suddenly the four vehicles swung off the road and swerved into a muddy farm field between the village and the riverbank, following each other at spaced intervals. Edge tracked their movement through the binoculars, holding his breath as a sickening knot of imminent dread tightened in the pit of his guts.

The four Mortar Carriers skidded in the mud, their tires biting deep into the soft grassy ground as they slewed their tails to the riverbank and braked to an urgent halt. Then the roof hatch doors on each vehicle burst open and the compartment space that housed the 120mm mortar filled with bustling crewmen. Within sixty seconds of frantic well-rehearsed activity the mortars were cleared and ready to fire.

Edge watched on with a sense of foreboding. The first Stryker sank on its suspension and a second later the echo of gunfire from the mortar tube carried across the plain. Edge saw a drifting wisp of haze and then turned his head to track the fall of shot. The mortar landed on the distant ridge and exploded in a thick billow of grey cloud.

"They're firing smoke," Edge growled. A split-second later the other three M1129's opened fire, the sound of each launch like a deep throaty cough.

One by one the smoke shells landed along the distant ridge line, blanketing the upper reaches of the crest in swirling clouds.

Then there was a deeper sound on the air; like the thunder of an approaching storm. Edge swung the binoculars back in the direction of the village and felt a surge of apprehension.

Far away but drawing quickly closer, appeared the column of Polish Wolverines and the Strykers of the 1st Squadron. They were racing down the road in a column, dragging behind them a skirt of dust and dirt.

"Here comes the Cavalry," Edge said. "Let's hope they're in time to – "

A sudden flurry of savage chattering noise choked off the rest of his sentence. Edge focused the binoculars back to the four mortar carriers. The crews were still hunched over their weapons, still working with mechanical urgency to feed their mortars, but now the long grass around the vehicles began fluttering as if fanned by a brisk breeze. Then there was a flash of sparks and the sound of ricochets.

"Machine guns!" Vince Waddingham seized Edge's shoulder and spun him urgently towards the Sypitki. "The Russians are dug in along the far side of the riverbank. Look!"

Long flickering tongues of flame identified the location of the two heavy machine gun emplacements.

Vince Waddingham snatched up the radio. "Checkmate Six Romeo, this is Bad Karma Xray. For Christ's sake, you have to order the mortar carriers back to the village! They're too close to the river. Do you read?"

But it was already too late. As Edge watched on helplessly, the Russian machine guns finally found their range and accuracy.

It sounded like heavy hail drumming on an iron roof. It was the noise of the Strykers coming under concentrated fire. A soldier in the nearest vehicle suddenly flung his arms in the air and arched his back. He stood frozen for a moment and then tumbled over the side of the vehicle and lay still in the grass. Another man sagged down on his knees clutching at his shoulder, and then a soldier in the far Stryker was struck full in the face. The impact sent his helmet spinning high in the air and disintegrated the man's head into red mist.

Edge watched on in agonized impotency, unable to do anything other than groan with frustration. Something low and fluttering caught his eye, moving like a darting bird in flight on a tiny tail of flame.

"Missile!"

The Russian Kornet anti-tank missile had been fired from the tree-covered crest on the far side of the river. It streaked across the field and struck the closest Stryker. The vehicle was completely engulfed in a ball of fire, and the roar of the explosion shook the air.

"Christ!" Vince Waddingham gasped.

A thick pall of smoke drifted on the breeze so that for long seconds the rest of the Mortar Carriers were obscured. When at last the haze cleared, Edge realized the surviving vehicles had stopped firing and were jouncing across the grass, fleeing desperately towards the built-up shelter of the village.

Only two of the Strykers escaped.

The trail vehicle was struck by a second Kornet anti-tank missile just as it ascended a low rise of ground, the impact so savage that it lifted the twenty-ton steel vehicle clear into the air as it blew apart. The sound of the explosion was like the toll of a doomsday bell. Twisted fragments of wreckage were thrown a hundred meters into the air and fell like rain across the field, starting small grass fires.

"Oh, God," Edge groaned.

But there was no time to mourn. The main attack was beginning.

Through billowing smoke, the Polish Wolverines came hurtling towards the bridge, driving headlong into the waiting Russian storm…

The Polish vehicles were flanked on either side of the road by two of Apache Troop's M1128 Mobile Gun System Strykers. The MGS's were the heavy-hitting hammers of the Cavalry Squadron – equipped with a 105mm cannon fed by an autoloader, and a 50cal machine gun that could be manually operated by the vehicle commander. The MGS had been specifically designed to support infantry and light vehicle operations. They braked to a sudden halt a hundred yards shy of the bridge on either side of the river, positioned like bodyguards to overwatch the assault.

The first Polish troop carrier hit the crossing at thirty kilometers an hour, charging down the center of the road. The vehicle reached the far side of the bridge before coming under machine gun fire. The Wolverine swerved onto the gravel and inexplicably stopped in a skidding billow of dirt. As the rear troop door swung open a Russian soldier rose to his feet from behind cover and fired an RPG. The front of the vehicle was engulfed in a fireball of oily smoke and flame. Incredibly, the soldiers inside the vehicle survived the devastating impact of the missile strike. They spilled out of the back of the Wolverine but were instantly cut down by Russian machine guns.

The following Wolverine exploded on the bridge, hit by two RPG's fired from close range. It disappeared behind a blistering wall of flames and was blown apart. Dead and injured soldiers were flung across the blacktop, some of the bodies thrashing feebly, their uniforms ablaze as they screamed and burned. Sporadic machine gun fire from the ridge whipped through the steel trusses, leaving bright silver scars on the grey painted metal.

The rest of the Polish vehicles spilled off the road and scattered into the nearby fields, looking for cover along the riverbank. Two of the Rosemaks slewed to a stop close to where Edge and the others lay, nosing themselves hull-down behind a hedge of bushes. The first vehicle opened fire with its

30mm cannon, shooting blindly across the river. The second vehicle launched smoke cannisters, blanketing the far bank of the Sypitki in grey swirling clouds. The rear doors of the Wolverines burst open and Polish troops scrambled into the long grass.

Within a matter of seconds the entire attack had stalled. The Wolverine in the center of the bridge was burning beneath a rising column of black oily smoke, and the roadway was strewn with broken bodies.

"Christ!" Edge groaned. "It's a disaster."

The two Stryker MGS's joined the battle. The vehicles were capable of firing six rounds a minute and carried four different types of ammunition in their auto-loaders. The commanders aboard both Strykers ordered canister loads and opened fire on the far ridge. The canister cartridges had a range of five hundred meters and were packed with hundreds of tungsten balls. They landed on the crest of the ridge and flailed through the woods like a mighty scythe, killing every Russian soldier within twenty yards and stripping the trees bare of foliage.

The vehicle commanders emerged from their hatches and opened fire with their 50cal machine guns, hosing the dense undergrowth that fringed the riverbank close to the bridge. The roar of each gun's vengeful fury seemed to dominate the battlefield so that momentum appeared to swing in the NATO troops favor – until one of the vehicle commanders was struck under the chin by a ricocheted round that deflected off the weapon's gun shield. He folded sideways in a pool of spreading blood.

Edge held his breath and watched the lead Stryker approach the bridge, moving cautiously, its 50cal firing through the onboard remote weapons station to lay down a hail of suppressing fire. Discarded shells rained on the road as the vehicle advanced, followed by a second Stryker in close support. The lead vehicle reached the burning remains of the Polish Wolverine and shouldered the ruins aside. With one lane of the bridge cleared, the two Strykers launched themselves at the crossing, running nose-to-tail into a wall of Russian counter-fire. Their objective was the shoulder of the road on the far side of the bridge. Neither Stryker made it. The first vehicle swerved to avoid dead bodies and was struck side-on by a Russian RPG fired from a roadside ditch. The crashing impact flipped the Stryker onto its side and engulfed it in smoke and roiling flames. Three of the soldiers inside the vehicle managed to scramble from the blazing ruin. They staggered amidst the wreckage, dazed and swaying. The Russians opened fire. One of the soldiers was struck in the shoulder. When the gunfire hit him, he stayed on his feet, tottering in a circle as the bullets slapped into his body. His arms flailed in the air and then he fell in a heap in the dust and did not move again. The second survivor sagged to his knees, clutching his chest. His head bowed so that he looked like a man in prayer – until the chattering roar of second machine gun flung him down into the dirt.

The last survivor from the wreckage tried to return fire. He began screaming; shouting with pain and horror. His face was a bloody mask. He fired blindly into the trees and then was cut down. He fell on his back, his heels drumming on the ground until he bled out.

The driver of the second Stryker braked to a skidding halt at the far end of the bridge and the vehicle's rear ramp crashed down. Soldiers spilled from the interior, their weapons raised as they ran into a hail of enemy resistance. They scattered across the blacktop and began to return sporadic fire. The Stryker lurched forward to clear the road for the rest of the armored column, but it was struck a glancing blow by an RPG. On fire and streaming smoke, the shattered hulk veered sideways out of control and tumbled down the grassy verge, into the river, killing the crew.

The battle quickly became a turmoil of noise, chaos and confusion. The Russians were dug in along the crest of the ridge and along the side of the road. The percussive clap of grenade explosions mingled with the incessant chatter of automatic fire until smoke and thunderous noise enveloped the battlefield. Bullets flayed the blacktop, filling the air with a rattling clamor of death.

The M1128's changed point of aim and concentrated their heavy machine gun fire on the ridge, fearful of friendly-fire casualties from continuing to strafe the riverbank. The vehicles magazines ran low on canister cartridges. The crews switched to HEAT rounds and directed their aim to the saddle of the ridge where the road intersected.

"We have to help the attack!" Edge clenched his jaw. "Come on. Follow me!"

Edge, Waddingham and Kalina dashed towards the bridge. The two Polish Wolverines by the riverbank sheltered them from enemy fire until they reached the roadside. The column of Cavalry Strykers were backed up for more than a mile. Some vehicles had disgorged their troopers to join the assault on the bridge and then veered into the fields along the riverbank to provide support fire. Others were stalled, their engines idling, waiting for the infantry to secure the crossing.

Edge scrambled up the rise and reached the roadside. The air was filled with the incessant hiss of gunfire and thick black smoke.

"Jesus!" he croaked. He dropped to one knee and waited for Waddingham to join him, then shouted at Kalina above the roar of battle. "Wait here!" he signaled with his hand to be certain she understood. "Wait for the rest of the infantry."

Edge and Waddingham dashed forward into the maelstrom.

The bridge was littered with empty shell casings, rubble, and twisted wreckage. They were enveloped in boiling smoke, but Edge knew that when they emerged beyond the wrecked troop carriers, they would be brutally exposed. He led Waddingham left, following the far guardrail while bullets plucked at the smokey veil and whizzed around them.

A fluke shift of wind drew the blanket of roiling smoke open like a theater curtain, revealing the horror of battle. Edge and Waddingham instinctively dropped to the ground, heads covered, stunned by the sudden hailstorm of fresh fire that swept the air above the bridge.

"Christ!" Edge gasped.

"It's a massacre! Everyone will be slaughtered."

They got to their feet and ran forward. The destroyed Wolverine in the center of the bridge had burned out, leaving a mangle of twisted wreckage and a black scar across the road. Edge ducked for cover behind the ruin and peered forward. He counted at least twenty American soldiers pinned down and under relentless fire. As he watched, a trooper on the far side of the bridge was hit in the face. The man had been tucked behind a steel upright. A bullet struck him flush in the cheek, and the wicked impact wrenched his head around. He seemed to be staring directly into Edge's eyes as his skull collapsed, and he fell face-first to the tarmac in a dark pool of blood.

Kalina emerged from the smoke behind them, weaving uncertainly across the road. Edge saw her and cursed bitterly. Waddingham reached out a huge hand and pulled her unceremoniously down to the ground as a flail of fresh bullets tore chunks from the blacktop. Edge gave Kalina a withering glare of rebuke and then exchanged a brief glance with Waddingham. "We can't stay here!" he growled. "We have to go forward."

Waddingham's expression was bleak but determined. A stray Russian bullet struck the wreckage of the Wolverine just an inch above his head. He flinched and cursed. "Okay," he nodded.

Edge tensed himself. He drew a deep breath – and together all three of them broke cover and charged into the fury of the firefight.

*

A dozen soldiers were crawling their way bravely across the blacktop, trying to reach the knot of survivors stranded at the far end of the bridge. The rest of the infantry huddled in the lee of the wrecked Wolverine that had been barged aside by the advancing Strykers. They were firing in short bursts at the ridgeline.

Edge went past them in a jinking run, crouched double to make himself small against the hail of gunfire sweeping across the bridge. Waddingham and Kalina followed in his footsteps. They dashed past two more soldiers who were sheltered behind smoldering debris, firing blindly into the trees. Edge pushed on, his jaw clenched, cursing the chattering machine guns and RPG's that had blunted the assault.

Ahead of him were the ruined carcasses of a Stryker and a Wolverine. Both vehicles had been mangled beyond recognition. Their blackened shells ghosted out of the swirling smoke as Edge dashed closer, drawn by the promise of temporary relief from the deadly fusillade. Edge reached the shelter of the overturned Stryker just as a grenade came skittering across the bridge. He threw himself into cover, but the grenade bounced across the blacktop and exploded harmlessly against the guardrail.

"Christ!" Edge gasped as Waddingham and Kalina pressed close to him.

"How much further to the end of the bridge?" Waddingham grunted.

Edge rolled onto his side and peeked around the edge of the ruined vehicle. He could see little through the smoke. He ducked back into cover just as a bullet zinged past his ear and ricocheted away.

"Fifteen yards," Edge guessed. He was panting, his face slick with sweat. He felt like he was trapped in a furnace. "We crawl from here."

He rolled onto his stomach and pushed on, Waddingham's strained breath hoarse behind him. Russian machine gun fire stitched a line across the tarmac, kicking up chunks of hot bitumen a few feet in front of Edge's face. He pressed his nose against the ground and covered his head with his hand. He could feel the vibration of the bullets as they gouged holes in the blacktop.

A loud commanding voice cut across the clamor of combat; a strident, booming voice barking orders to the stranded soldiers. Edge looked sideways. A tall Cavalry Captain stood amidst the smoke, waving men forward, urging troopers on. Edge watched with incredulity while enemy fire flew thick through the air.

The Captain lead the renewed attack with a calm, unflustered assurance, and behind him surged a fresh wave of grimly determined infantry. All along the tree-covered ridge the roar of automatic fire hammered, the flames spat and explosions roared.

Edge got to his feet and joined the assault. His bulky equipment thumped against him as he ran, and sweat poured down his face.

'Wait!" Waddingham dashed into the open with Kalina at his elbow. Almost immediately the attack began to falter, losing momentum as the lead troops ran into a murderous fury of Russian fire.

"Keep going!" the tall Cavalry Captain cried. A shell – fired from God-knows where – struck the river beside the bridge and a great plume of brown water deluged them. Through the skeins of swirling smoke Edge could see the end of the bridge and a wink of flickering orange flame. He braced himself for the impact of a bullet, but it never came. Instead the man beside him threw up his arms and staggered. He had been shot in the pelvis. His legs buckled and he fell to the ground, smearing the road with his blood and gore. Edge leaped a tangle of debris and Waddingham loomed up on his shoulder.

"Get to the end of the bridge!"

Two Polish soldiers and a trooper from one of the destroyed Strykers lay sprawled on the blacktop. The Polish militia had been badly burned, their bodies blackened and charred. The Cavalry trooper had been shot in the guts and had dragged himself across the bridge before dying. Edge saw the slick wet trail he left behind as the life seeped from him. A bullet whipped past Edge's face and hit another man in the thigh. The soldier clutched at his leg and crumpled to the ground.

"Carry him!" the Cavalry Captain shouted to the troops following. Others were not so lucky. One of the charging men crawled to a steel bridge truss with a shattered bleeding leg trailing behind him. Another, his face a horror mask of blood from a gruesome head wound, clawed at his eyes with his hands and staggered blindly into the open. He was screaming in pain. The Russians cut him down.

Edge choked on thick smoke and doubled over, retching. Waddingham seized his arm.

"Are you hit? Are you hit?"

Edge shook his head, his eyes streaming oily tears. Kalina loomed out of the smoke and flinched as a bullet whizzed past her face and struck a steel beam.

Then the tall Cavalry Captain was beside them. He seized Edge by the collar of his grimy sweat-stained uniform. "Are you injured soldier?"

Edge shook his head. "No, sir."

"Then keep moving! We've got to get across this bridge and find cover."

"There is no cover," Edge ducked instinctively as a bullet cracked past his head.

"How do you know?"

"I'm a scout," Edge had to shout above the roar of the battle. "I was here before sunrise. I walked to the far side of the bridge. The only shelter is along the slope of the riverbank."

The Captain narrowed his eyes and regarded Edge carefully. "Who the hell are you?"

"Sergeant Tom Edge, 2nd Platoon, Outlaw Troop, 4th Squadron."

"Captain Matthew Walker," the Cavalry officer introduced himself.

"I wish I could say it was a pleasure, sir," Edge said bitterly. He felt uncomfortably exposed, aware that any moment a torrent of machine gun fire could cut them down. Indifferent to the risk, Captain Walker fearlessly drew himself upright and filled his lungs. Bullets bounced off a steel bridge truss a few feet from where he stood, but the Captain seemed not to notice. Instead he peered hard into the chaos and bellowed.

"Troopers! Follow me! Make for the riverbank!"

Walker and Edge started to run. Waddingham and Kalina broke cover and joined the dash. Captain Walker continued to bark orders, waving his arms and urging the rest of the survivors to join the desperate charge. Edge glanced over his shoulder, appalled at what he saw. The bridge was a slaughterhouse of spattered blood, broken bodies and fire-blackened carnage.

The ragged knot of cursing, frightened men rushed past the last of the steel trusses and their boots crunched on loose gravel. Edge swerved off the road and threw himself to the right. He crashed through a thorn bush and tumbled down the muddy slope of the riverbank. He was panting – trembling with fatigue and exhaustion – as the rest of the survivors dived beneath the dip of the bank and into cover.

*

Edge clambered up the muddy slope and peered through a clump of leafy shrubs that grew dense along the riverbank. He was covered from sight, but not from gunfire. A Russian mortar shell burst close by and sprayed clods of earth over his back.

"It's a slaughterhouse," Edge watched on in horror as more men fought their way across the bridge.

Two more Strykers were nosing cautiously forward, their machine guns blazing suppressing fire while, sheltered in their shadow, infantry followed close behind. When the first Stryker reached the bottleneck in the middle of the bridge, it came under sudden attack from somewhere unseen along the ridgeline.

All Edge heard was a ground-rumbling roar and then a mighty explosion. The Stryker was struck front-on and dissolved into a fireball. The impact shunted the vehicle backwards and ripped it apart. The soldiers sheltered behind the Stryker were killed or maimed by flying shrapnel and the flames that swept over them. The massive roar of the explosion stunned the battlefield into several seconds of relative silence. Then the terrible screams of the wounded began. As Edge watched on, one soldier was flung through the air and over the bridge rail into the river below. Another trooper caught fire. He shrieked in excruciating agony as the flames engulfed him, thrashing his hands feebly until he collapsed on the ground. Another trooper had his leg cleanly severed above the knee. Rivulets of blood and gore dripped from the steel trusses of the bridge and stained the surface of the Sypitki River brown.

Through it all, the fire from the Russian machine guns never relented, piling up bodies and broken vehicles across the bridge so that the living had to clamber over the dead and dying.

Edge turned away, aghast, and looked about him for Vince Waddingham. He found him kneeling in the mud by the water's edge, wrapping a field dressing around Kalina's hand. Edge slid down the embankment.

"Are you hurt?" he asked the Polish woman.

"Just shrapnel," Waddingham answered for her. But there were many other wounded close by, some groaning softly in pain, others screaming shrilly, demented with agony. One man lay on his back, his jacket ripped open, trying futilely to hold his entrails inside his stomach while two soldiers, covered in blood up to their elbows, fought to keep him alive. Other men sat numb and dazed, their eyes unfocussed. Their bodies shook in uncontrollable spasms, like men in the grips of fever. The sounds of their agonized cries were blurred by chanted prayers and frantic calls for help.

"Bill? Where the fuck are you?"

"3rd Platoon on me! On *me*, dammit!"

"Christ almighty! Give me something for the pain!"

"Quick! Find me a field dressing before he bleeds out."

Edge scrambled back up the riverbank with Waddingham and Kalina at his side. He found himself lying in the mud beside the Cavalry Captain who had led the charge.

Captain Walker poked his head up, and peered carefully through a thicket of thorny bush. His face was smeared in dirt and grime but his eyes were bright and intense. He studied the far ridge for a long minute and then ducked back down behind cover as a flurry of machine gun bullets whipped overhead, shredding leaves and twigs from the bushes.

There were around fifty soldiers strewn along the riverbank. It was a paltry force and they were pinned down by enemy fire. Over his shoulder Walker saw the bridge was blocked by burning wreckage. Men were trying to rig a tow line to the stricken vehicles to clear a way forward. The troopers were working in the open, under heavy fire, while dismounted soldiers nearby provided cover. Walker realized there would be no rescue from across the river; his small force was cut off from help.

"The bastards are dug in deep right across the ridge and along the roadside," Captain Walker declared. "But until we give the Russians something to think about, hundreds more men are going to die clearing that bridge. We have to create a distraction to buy our guys time to mount a fresh attack."

He lifted his head once more and surveyed the ground in front of them. Beyond a stretch of grassy field stood the fringe of a dense thicket of woods. The tree line followed the gentle curve of the road, rising to the low saddle of the ridge and was cordoned off by an old barbed-wire fence that sagged on weathered posts.

Walker grabbed Edge's sleeve and pulled him close. The wind of a bullet whipped past Edge's cheek, so close that he flinched away instinctively.

"See that barbed wire fence?"

"Yes, Captain."

"It runs all the way along the verge of the road as far as the dip in the ridgeline."

Edge said nothing.

"And see the fringe of the woods?"

Edge looked. The line of trees stood sixty or seventy paces away across broken open ground.

"There's no fire coming from the trees. The Russians are on the ridge and along the road, but we can threaten their flank if we can get into those woods."

"You want to charge across sixty yards of open ground?"

Captain Walker gave a thin, defiant smile. "Sergeant, my daddy always told me that it's better to die on your feet than live on your knees. If we don't fight back we're going to die here in the mud. Sooner or later the Russians will pick us off, or they'll hammer us with mortars…"

Edge studied the open ground more carefully. Sixty yards; eight to ten seconds of exposure, running towards a hail of Russian machine gun fire. "Okay."

The word was passed along the line and men took a moment to check their weapons, to say prayers and steel their resolve. Edge wondered whether the anxious terror he felt was the same fear the heroes from the First Great War experienced the moment before they sprang from their trenches to charge across no-man's land. Beside him Vince Waddingham looked pale. Kalina seemed small and withdrawn with silent fear.

Suddenly Captain Walker dropped down beside them again, crouched like a sprinter on the blocks with an M4 in his hands. He looked left and right one final time. "Come on!" he roared and clambered over the rim of the riverbank.

Edge, Waddingham, Kalina, and most of the other soldiers rose up from the mud and followed. Edge ran hard, his elbows pumping, his heart hammering in his chest. For the first few seconds they ran into eerie silence. Then a Russian machine gunner on the ridge saw them and all hell broke loose.

The ground around the running men erupted in chunks of flung dirt and clods of grass as the machine gun drew a bead on the lead figures and opened fire. Edge jinked left, running alongside Waddingham. He could hear Kalina's panting breath close behind him. He was pacing himself; using his body to shield her from direct fire. A flail of machine gun bullets lashed them like wind-driven hail.

Captain Walker was halfway across the meadow when he staggered suddenly and lost his step. His knees buckled, but he came upright again and ran on for ten more paces – then collapsed in the grass.

"Christ!" Edge swore. He tossed his M4 to Waddingham and heaved the Captain to his feet. The man's face was pallid and waxen. Edge felt warm blood soak through the fabric of his jacket. "He's been hit in the chest. Vince! Vince, cover us!"

Edge slung the dead-weight of the Captain's body over his shoulder in a fireman's carry and stared indecisively for a moment. They were stranded in the middle of the field and under increasingly heavy fire from the Russians. A second machine gun had joined the hunt and men all around them were falling.

"Which way?" Waddingham snapped.

"Back!" Edge said. "Get back to the riverbank."

The attack was finished.

Some of the nearby men heard the call and they hesitated, then began to retreat. Others raced on towards the tree line and were cut down. Edge ran until his knees sagged and his feet felt leaden. He ran until his eyes stung with sweat and his lungs burned, expecting each step to be his last. Then the ground gave way beneath him and he fell in an awkward tumble down the muddy slope.

Behind them the field was strewn with the freshly dead and dying. Some men clawed at the grass to pull themselves forward, leaving wet red streaks of blood across the ground. Some simply lay and stared up at the vastness of the sky as the life faded from them. Others cried out in sobbing, hysterical agony, and the sound of their slow despairing deaths tortured the nerves of the stunned survivors who were helpless to aid them.

Edge collapsed and rolled onto his back, his chest heaving, gagging and husking for breath. Kalina and Waddingham ripped the wounded man's jacket open and went to urgent work. Captain Walker had been shot high on the right side of the chest. Waddingham guessed the collar bone had been broken. They rolled him on to his side and Kalina probed the exit wound with her finger. Captain Walker groaned in pain but did not cry out. He gritted his teeth, then sagged back in a spreading pool of his own bright blood.

"He's gonna make it," Waddingham declared, then worked quickly to treat and bandage the wound. Edge sat up. He felt dazed, his senses numbed by the deafening noise of the battle. Barely a dozen troopers had survived the aborted attack.

Edge blinked his eyes. "But will we?"

Chapter 5:

With Raven RQ-11 tactical drones circling high above the battlefield, Lieutenant Colonel Sutcliffe and Major Nowakowski were able to watch the bridge crossing in real time from the security of the TOC. Two monitors stood on a tabletop relaying color images as well as readouts of data and a compass display.

Sutcliffe sat grim-faced and fuming. To this point the crossing had been an abject failure. He scowled at the monitors as the Raven drones turned lazy circles in the sky to reveal the wreckage-torn bridge and a rising column of black smoke. The crossing was impassable until the destroyed vehicles that blocked the route were cleared away. There were dozens of dead bodies littered across the blacktop and more in the river, floating downstream. The two destroyed Mortar Carriers still burned in the field by the village so that the entire skyline seemed smudged by smoke.

Russian infantry, armed with cheap RPG's, had stunted the attack in just a few frantic seconds. Now the Cavalry had a bloody brutal fight on their hands.

Major Nowakowski too was mortified by the savage damage the Russians had inflicted on the spearhead of the column. Two of his valuable Wolverines had been blown apart with contemptible ease. He paced the TOC tent restlessly, his arms folded, his features crumpled with concern. He had insisted the glory of being the first across the Sypitki be given to his Polish troops. Now they were all dead.

As one of the drones swept east of the bridge, Sutcliffe saw the handful of survivors that were marooned along the far riverbank and his frustration turned to rage. He began barking a string of rapid-fire orders to his aides.

"Dammit, get the rest of the MGS's into the fight," he said. "Move them forward and to the flanks. I want fire support here and here," he stabbed his finger at the monitor. "And I want forward support vehicles with towing equipment on that bridge within five minutes. We've got to clear the wreckage, asap!"

He got to his feet, knocking over the chair and stomped out into the daylight. He could smell smoke from the battlefield drifting on the air and hear the far-away rumble of heavy gunfire and explosions. He drew a deep breath and tried to clear his mind but the images of so many destroyed vehicles and dead soldiers haunted him; compelled him to set aside his bitter frustration and focus on a solution.

He strode back into the TOC tent with his features fixed and his mind made up. "We're not leaving those men on the far bank to be slaughtered. We're going to punch through," he addressed every officer and aide in the room. "Get in touch with Comanche Troop. It's their turn to take up the fight. And before we go forward this time I want that ridgeline blown to hell, understand? Pour everything we've got onto that god-damned crest until there isn't a tree left standing."

On the battlefield, the Strykers of Comanche Troop moved forward, led by their three M1128 MGS's which swerved to the east and found hull-down cover behind undulating ground well back from the river. Their canister cartridges were well out of range, so the vehicle commanders ordered HEAT rounds loaded and the 105mm guns began to bombard the far ridge.

For ten unrelenting minutes the M1128's pounded the enemy's positions until the sun turned eerily red behind a pall of smoke and dust, and the world seemed trapped in a permanent twilight. Under the cover of the bombardment and smoke a Combat Recovery Team moved on to the bridge to tow the wrecked Wolverine and Stryker carcasses away. They were defended by a swarm of infantry who had orders only to protect the recovery operation. They laid down a withering wall of suppressing fire from their M249 SAWs and small arms, concentrating their efforts on the verge of the road at the far end of the bridge and the clumps of bush that were strung along the riverbank to the west.

Only one brave Russian dared show himself, leaping up from of a shallow trench by the roadside to fire an RPG. The man was cut down by American fire and the missile flew wide of its target.

Finally the Strykers of Comanche Troop rolled forward, their cargo of soldiers deployed behind each vehicle as they jounced warily onto the bridge. There was still a great litter of tangled wreckage and debris strewn across the blacktop, and many of the dead had not been recovered. The roadway was slathered in gruesome streaks of blood and glittered with thousands of spent shells.

The first two Strykers reached the mid-point without meeting resistance. In the background the M1128's continued to pound the far ridge, and the relentless fury of suppressing fire the Americans directed along the roadside forced the Russian defenders deep into their entrenched positions. But then a thunderous 'crack!' split the fragile tension and the lead Stryker disintegrated into a firestorm of flames and boiling smoke. The shock of the explosion rolled across the sky and in its wake left a dozen soldiers dead on the roadway and a dozen more seriously injured. Their cries of agony cut through the sudden stunned silence and presaged another murderous wave of fighting.

Sitting in the TOC, his eyes glued anxiously to the monitors, Lieutenant Colonel Sutcliffe gave a gut-sickened groan of bleak realization. "Oh, Christ," he moaned softly. "The Russians have got tanks."

*

"Go! Go! Go!" an officer on the bridge shouted. He was bleeding from a shrapnel cut to the forearm, grimacing in pain and dripping blood on his boots. He waved the infantry forward, his voice strident.

The soldiers fired as they sprinted gallantly into the maelstrom of smoke and danger. Some men mouthed silent prayers while others gritted their teeth and tried not to cry out in fear. One soldier dropped his M4 and it clattered on the road. Another man spat a wad of chewing tobacco then leaped a dead body and dropped to his knee to fire at the ridgeline. The leading infantry could see through the whorls of smoke that the route to the far side of the bridge was barricaded with twisted wreckage and mounds of dead bodies. The Russian infantry sprang from their trenches and unleashed a fresh hell of gunfire that filled the air with death.

The American troopers pressed on, running at a crouch, weaving from small cover to small cover. Their heavy kit flapped and rattled about their bodies as they moved.

Then, at last, more Strykers bumped onto the bridge, belching black smoke as their drivers gunned the engines in a reckless dash to reach the far side of the river. The lead vehicle fired smoke cannisters that obliterated the winding road and the ridge from sight, and then dashed forward at high speed. Dead bodies and twisted metal debris loomed out of the haze as dull dark shapes. Then came the drumming hail of ricochets as the first vehicle ran into a storm of sprayed light arms and machine gun fire. The vehicle swerved then straightened, its own 50cal machine gun adding to the wild clamor of rattling chaos.

The first Stryker reached the far side of the bridge and swung off the road, knocking down an old wire fence and ploughing into a tall stand of trees. A Russian soldier carrying an RPG dashed forward from out of the shadows. The crew inside the Stryker recognized the danger and the vehicle's 50cal machine gun hunted the man. Through a withering hail of gunfire, the Russian fired a snap shot into the haze, but missed. The rocket flew wide and disappeared on a tail of smoke and fireworks into the chaos and confusion.

The Stryker's 50cal machine gun traversed and cut the Russian down.

A dozen troopers burst out of the smoke, following the Stryker. They dashed across the road to the foot of the crest and dropped into shallow ditches. The ground had been churned by canister fire; the trees and shrubs flensed of their foliage. There were dead Russian bodies in the trenches, the soft earth muddied by their blood. The Americans began shooting at targets further up the rise, but they were overwhelmed by a storm of heavy machine gun fire. One man was hit in the neck and screamed in shock and agony until he bled out. Another trooper had half his guts shot away. He sat down in the trench with his legs stretched before him and muttered a string of silent curses until death took him.

The Stryker reversed out of the trees and rolled back onto the road, it's 50cal still firing short bursts along the ridgeline. Another Stryker emerged through the smoke, two of its huge tires deflated and on fire as it careened into a roadside ditch. A Russian mortar shell landed on the riverbank, throwing up an avalanche of dirt and dust and debris.

It was imperative that the Americans move quickly to consolidate their tenuous bridgehead on the far side of the river. Two more Strykers dashed forward, their own machine guns adding to the fury while in their wake troopers charged bravely forward as if the hounds of Hell were at their heels.

For a brief moment it seemed the bridge that had been paid for with so much spilled blood was finally won. The charging Strykers reached the far bank of the river and dashed heedlessly along the road, racing past the vehicle that had crashed into the trees. The road appeared open to the Americans, rising gradually as it bent to the left.

Two thunderous *'cracks!'* spaced just ten seconds apart turned triumph into defeat. The first Stryker blew apart in an eruption of flying metal and flame. The second Stryker was struck side on as it reached the bend in the road. The crashing impact blew the vehicle over onto its roof, wheels spinning crazily as the shattered steel carcass became engulfed in smoke.

The infantry that followed the Strykers had been left behind by their mad dash down the road. The soldiers flung themselves to the ground. One man lay twitching in the dirt in a pool of his own blood, but the rest were uninjured.

"Fall back!" someone shouted. He sounded like he was sobbing.

"Get back across the bridge!"

The battlefield smelled of blood and smoke and fear. The suppressing fire from the American machine guns fell suddenly silent. The M1128's had fired at the crest of the ridge until they had no more ammunition in their autoloader magazines. Now the bridge was wreathed in so much smoke there were no more visible targets. One American trooper, his left arm severed by flying shrapnel, staggered out of the maelstrom and stood in a numb, swaying daze. He had dropped his weapon and lost his helmet. His face was streaked with sweat. He shuffled into the open and stood on buckling knees, bewildered and panting, until a Russian sniper shot him dead.

The wicked retort of the shot seemed to galvanize the stranded infantry into action. They started to edge backwards. When Russian machine guns began to hunt them down, their panic became absolute.

"Get back!"

"Break cover! Run for it!"

The moment they scrambled to their feet and began retreating, Russians along the ridgeline opened fire. One trooper screamed his defiance and emptied his weapon's magazine into the nearby trees until the ground around him erupted in a flail of gouged dirt and hissing bullets. He dropped to his knees, bleeding from several wounds. He continued firing but he was silent now, his mouth hanging open, his weapon swinging wildly until he disappeared behind the crashing eruption of a mortar shell strike.

*

"God damn it!" Lieutenant Colonel Sutcliffe punched the table as he watched the ignominious retreat on monitors at the TOC, eight miles behind the battlefront. He bounced to his feet and paced the floor, his features tight with bitter frustration. In the corner of the tent, Major Nowakowski stood, glowering. He stepped forward at last. His voice quivered with loathing.

"This fiasco," he stabbed his finger at the monitor, "is all the fault of your scout who reconnoitered the crossing. Sergeant Edge should be court-martialed for dereliction of duty and cowardly negligence. If he had done his work thoroughly, Colonel Sutcliffe, none of this would have happened."

Sutcliffe withered the Polish Major to silence with a steely glare. "Edge did his job. And regardless of what he reported, we were still obliged to take the bridge. Nothing in his intelligence changed our attack."

Nowakowski looked like he had more to say. Sutcliffe wasn't in the mood. The American had made all the accommodations to polite diplomacy he was prepared to make. He turned his back on the Major and hunched over the table for a few more long moments of futile despair. The infantry that had reached the far side of the river had now either retreated back to safety or were lying dead on the blacktop. All that remained on the far bank were the destroyed carcasses of several Strykers and the knot of survivors still stranded along the riverbank. In the background the radio was a chaos of accidental transmissions of gunfire, desperate shouting, frantic commands and pleading cries for support. The troops at the battlefront were too busy fighting for their lives to follow radio etiquette so that outbreaks of desperation overwhelmed legitimate command orders.

Sutcliffe tried to match the radio chatter blaring through the speakers with the grainy images he saw displayed on the monitors. Comanche Troop had been badly mauled by the tenacious ferocity of the Russian defenders. Their attack had been savaged and repulsed. Some of the troops on the front line appeared numbed and shocked. Some were cowering in cover while others sheltered behind the log-jam of vehicles stalled by the roadside. Closer to the riverbank it looked like men were digging defensive positions and foxholes.

"I'm going forward to the battlefront," the Colonel announced to the 1st Squadron's Executive Officer. He couldn't command the conflict from behind the lines. He needed to be at the bridge to transform the milling chaos into renewed purpose. "Get me a Humvee and a driver."

Sutcliffe sat up front in the passenger seat. Major Nowakowski and the S-3 Operations Officer clambered into the back. The vehicle sped away in a skid of dirt and gravel.

It took just a few minutes to reach the front. As the Humvee drew closer, the smoke became thicker and the sounds of sporadic gunfire and mortar explosions louder. They reached the tail of the Stryker column, and Sutcliffe urged the driver on towards the bridge. The American vehicles were stalled on the shoulder of the road, parked askew with their ramps down and their cargoes of infantry sitting idly in the long grass.

Closer to the bridge the scene became one of confusion and destruction. The driver parked the Humvee and Sutcliffe strode towards a knot of officers gathered around the rear of a Troop command vehicle. The men's faces were haggard and smeared with dirt and sweat. One officer stood barking rapid-fire orders to a harried radio operator. Someone spotted Sutcliffe and the men snapped to attention. Sutcliffe waved their salutes away with a brusque swat of his hand.

"Sitrep," he demanded.

The officer who had been shouting orders straightened. He was the commander of Comanche Troop. His eyes were bloodshot and his face wrenched into a bleak grimace. "The Russians have at least one, maybe two tanks hull-down by the side of the road," the office spoke quickly. "We haven't spotted them yet, but they're there, probably on the rise where the road passes through the saddle of the ridge. They're battering everything we send across the river."

Sutcliffe grunted. The air was filled with swirling dust and smoke. A mortar shell landed fifty yards away, throwing up an eruption of dirt and debris. The soldiers flinched instinctively. Major Nowakowski cringed and seemed to shrink away. He moved until he was standing in the shelter of a Stryker, still in earshot of the Colonel as he fired off questions.

"Losses?"

"Heavy, sir. The infantry has been hammered, and we've lost upwards of half-a-dozen Strykers."

The Colonel took a moment to make sense of the chaos, walking towards the bridge with the cluster of staff officers trailing him. He seemed contemptuous of the danger, ignoring the staccato rattle of enemy machine gun fire. A Russian shell landed on the riverbank and flung a geyser of mud and water into the air. Sutcliffe snatched up a pair of binoculars and scanned the bridge. The smoke had thinned enough so that he could make out the horrific destruction clearly. The bodies of the soldiers not yet recovered lay in crumpled heaps, and near the middle of the bridge, where the fighting had been fiercest, they were stacked in careless bloody mounds between the burned-out ruins of several Strykers.

"We have to attack in force," Sutcliffe assessed the situation. So far the Strykers had crossed the bridge in wary pairs and been picked off by Russian RPG's, but now most of the enemy fire seemed to be coming from the ridge. "And I want the rest of the Squadron's MGS's brought into the battle. I want every gun we have aimed at the saddle of that crest. Everything, understand?"

One of the officers following the Colonel nodded and scurried back to the command vehicle to issue orders.

The Russians chose the moment to launch a barrage of mortar shells and the sound of the cacophony was like an echoing clap of doom. The noise became a deafening percussive assault that melded into an endless thunder. A soldier standing just twenty yards away from the Colonel was snatched away in an explosion of blood. Skeins of choking dust hung in the air, thick as smoke.

Through the clamor of the bombardment a curious far-away whine seemed to float on the air, barely discernable above the ground rumbling crash of explosions. It sounded like a wavering echo that persisted, growing louder.

"Incoming!" a sharp-eyed soldier pointed into the sky.

"Enemy aircraft! Take cover!"

The Su-25 appeared from behind the far ridge, flying low and fast. The Frogfoot was the mainstay of Russian '*shturmovoy*' ground-attack regiments. It was the approximate equivalent of the American A-10 Warthog. The aircraft had been designed as a tank killer that specialized in providing close air support to troops on a battlefield, and it had seen combat action in every major theatre of conflict since the '80's.

The aircraft was armed with sixteen AT-16 *Vikhr* anti-tank missiles suspended from its wing pods and a 30mm cannon.

The Su-25 flashed over the battlefield, flying just a few hundred feet above the ground, and unleashed its entire payload into the long stationary column of American vehicles. The missiles leaped off their rails in a blinding flare of flames and sparks, and flew like arrows towards the tangled traffic jam of Strykers. The AT-16's darted over the bridge littered with dead bodies and ruined burned out vehicles... over the river that was stained with blood and strewn with corpses... over the heads of the American soldiers who milled around the riverbank – and then plunged down at last into the Squadron of vehicles. Suddenly the battlefield filled with a fresh thunder of massive explosions. Shrapnel whistled through the air and the ground seemed to erupt. Chunks of burning debris were hurled hundreds of feet into the sky and then fell like hail. The noise was a deafening numbing crescendo fit for the end of the world. Men were thrown to the ground. Others were immolated in the blasts. A bloom of bright orange fireballs billowed into the sky. Dust and debris blanketed the battlefield. Black oily smoke blotted out the sun.

The first murderous attack was over in just a few seconds. The Russian Su-25 turned in a tight circle over the village and roared back, its twin engines at full military power and its lethal 30mm cannon spitting flame. Troopers that just moments before had been waiting idly in the grassy fields scrambled desperately for cover. Some men fired their M4's at the Su-25 as it flashed overhead like a hunting bird of prey.

One alert trooper made a desperate dash across the road and drew a shoulder-launched Stinger missile system from the interior of a Stryker. He powered up the system and aimed the missile at the Su-25 just as the aircraft began climbing out of its strafing run. When the seeker system locked on to the Russian aircraft, the Stinger made a distinctive sound. The trooper squeezed the trigger and a small rocket shot the missile out of the launch tube. Then the main solid rocket engine ignited. The Stinger flashed across the sky at Mach 2 trailing a tail of white smoke.

The Stinger's passive IR/UV sensors tracked the Su-25 by locking on to the infrared heat signature produced by the aircraft's engines.

The missile struck the Russian ground attack aircraft as it began to change course to the south east. The plane erupted in flames, and a heartbeat later the sound of the explosion filled the air. The Su-25 fell from the sky as burning debris. The soldiers on the ground gave a ragged cheer. It was a small triumph, but it did not compensate for the nightmare of destruction the Su-25 left in its wake. Six Strykers had been struck and destroyed in the attack, and fifty men killed or injured.

Major Nowakowski had been flung to the ground during the missile strike. Blood splashed his tunic and sprayed his face. He cried out in appalled horror.

"Good God! I have been struck! Help me! Help me someone, please. I am badly wounded."

Dust-covered soldiers went to his aid. They hauled the Major upright. "You're not hit," one of the soldiers made a rudimentary inspection and could find no injuries. "It's not your blood – it's his."

Swaying on his feet, his ears ringing and his senses numbed, Major Nowakowski stared mutely at the corpse of a Lieutenant whose chest had been blown open by the blast. The man had been standing on the outer circle of Colonel Sutcliffe's aides and had inadvertently shielded the Major from the horrendous impact of the explosions.

More men ran to where Colonel Sutcliffe lay. He was in the dirt on his back, his chest soaked in warm spreading blood.

One of the soldiers shook Sutcliffe's shoulder and shouted, his voice thick with alarm.

"Sir! Sir! Can you hear me?"

Sutcliffe was bleeding from a chest wound. His face was ashen and there was more blood on his neck, soaking the collar of his uniform. Two men gingerly lifted him to his feet. Sutcliffe clamped his hand over the wound and sagged forward so he leaned, almost doubled over. He stood like that, his features wracked with pain, and his voice sounded thick and gasping.

"Pull everyone back from the bridge. Disengage immediately."

"But sir!" the Squadron's Operation's Officer protested. "We've worn the Russians down. Resistance from machine gun fire and hand-held anti-tank weapons has been suppressed close to the river. I know we can force a bridgehead with just one more concerted push."

"I said fall back, immediately!" Sutcliffe growled. His breath rattled in his chest and he took a tottering step to keep his balance. A medic arrived wearing blood-covered rubber gloves. "Stretcher!"

Before Sutcliffe could be carried from the battlefield, the S-3 tried one last time to salvage the attack. "Colonel, if we pull back now, everyone and everything we have lost in this fight will have been for nothing. Sir! That bridge is soaked in American blood. The men died trying to force a bridgehead. We owe it to them to continue trying. With one well-coordinated push we can overwhelm the enemy armor and force a victory."

"Damn it! I said disengage!"

"The Colonel is right," Major Nowakowski said. His face was ashen, his eyes dulled with shock. He was scared. His hands trembled and his voice quavered. The attack by the Russian Su-25 had terrified him. "The enemy are deeply entrenched and they have tanks defending the road. There is nothing we can do with armored troop carriers against such force. We must call in our own air strikes. Until then any further attempt to force a crossing is suicidal folly."

It was over.

The attack to seize the bridge over the Sypitki had failed.

*

At first Edge thought the Strykers were preparing for a fresh attack, then he thought Command was massing the MGS's to bombard the ridge, then he speculated the assault would be from the infantry this time. Finally, as the wind picked up and the sounds of machine gun fire began to wane, he realized that there was no imminent attack, and that the smoke was being fired to conceal a withdrawal.

Behind a dense curtain of grey haze, the American and Polish armored troop carriers retreated from the battlefield. The M1128 MGS's were the last to leave, remaining to provide overwatch until the final Stryker withdrew.

Edge watched the ignominious retreat from the muddy slope of the far riverbank, his eyes wide with slow dawning horror.

"They're abandoning us," Captain Walker groaned.

"Jesus!" Vince Waddingham stared into the shifting veil of smoke. "Do you think it's some kind of tactical feint?"

"No." Edge turned and gazed at the Russian-held ridge. Through the skeins of swirling mist, he could see that the crestline had been completely denuded of trees and foliage. It remined him of a World War 1 battlefield. Broken, blackened tree stumps dotted the ragged ground.

"We've been left for dead!" Kalina's voice filled with horror and disbelief.

It was a disaster. For several more minutes they stared into the opaque greyness, looking for signs that the Squadron's Strykers were forming up to resume the fight, or that infantry were massing beyond the bridge, preparing to rush the crossing. Nothing moved. The sounds of rumbling engines grew fainter. The gunfire died to a faltering staccato and then stopped abruptly. They had been forsaken.

There were a dozen survivors, clinging to the muddy slope of the riverbank, many of them injured. They were all that remained of the ill-fated attempt to reach the cover of the trees. Between them they had a handful of M4's, a few spare magazines of ammunition and maybe twenty grenades; not enough to turn back a determined attempt to overwhelm them.

Not that the Russians even needed to mount an attack. They could simply pound the Americans into submission with mortar fire, hammering the river's edge with a bombardment of explosions until either the stranded men were all dead, or beaten into dazed surrender.

Two of the troopers went from man to man, salvaging spare weapons, grenades and ammunition from the dead and the seriously wounded. Someone handed around cold MRE's and a canteen of water. With a small start, Edge realized how thirsty he was. He drank his fill and passed the canteen to Kalina.

Edge considered their position and his mood grew dark. There was no hope of escape to the west – that would mean crawling along the riverbank, passing beneath the bridge, and then exposing themselves to Russian fire from the ridge. He turned and looked east. The riverbank was about eight feet of sloping mud and stone, fringed by a low natural wall of shrubs. But he could see no position that could be defended. The river ran in a relatively straight line for about a mile before kinking out of sight. What lay beyond the bend Edge did not know, but he doubted so many wounded could be moved safely without arousing Russian attention. He swore uselessly.

The river was about sixty feet wide, flowing east on a strong current. The water's edge was overgrown with wild reeds, clumps of long grass and stunted gnarled trees. Closer to the bridge grew a high stand of green bulrushes. There were bodies of dead American soldiers snagged in the reeds, floating face down in the brown water.

The sight of the bobbing, stranded corpses seemed to deepen Edge's despair. He had a dozen injured soldiers and they were marooned on a riverbank, surrounded by Russian troops, with no hope of rescue and not enough weapons to defend themselves.

Edge suspected that he, Waddingham and Kalina could escape – either by waiting until dark and making another attempt for the woods, or by quickly following the riverbank east, evading capture before the Russians could organize themselves and come down from the ridge to confront them. But what of the injured?

And if they were captured while trying to escape the Russians, what would be the consequences? If they surrendered themselves now; if they threw down their weapons and rose from cover with their hands held high, most likely they would end up in a prisoner of war camp.

Edge ran his eyes over the miserable haggard faces of the survivors and grimaced. Only a couple of the men were uninjured. The rest were badly wounded. Most of them had stomach and leg wounds. One man had his forehead swaddled in grubby blood-stained bandages. He was muttering to himself in a feverish delirium, his hands fluttering like dying birds at his side. He had been shot in the back of the head. He was unlikely to survive the hour. There were others in a similar state; two Apache Troop soldiers who had been amongst the first to cross the bridge were now clinging to life. One man had been shot in the neck. His breathing was shallow and his pulse weak. His buddy had been hit in the groin by flying shrapnel. He lay in a pool of spreading blood and mud and whimpered softly. Neither would live to see another day. Other men were nursing broken bones and heavily bandaged wounds. Barely half of the survivors could fire a weapon if the Russians decided to launch an assault.

"We don't know if the Squadron is coming back to mount a fresh attack," Edge leaned close to Waddingham and Kalina and kept his voice low. "They could be calling in an air strike…"

"Unlikely," Captain Walker interrupted. His voice was tight with pain from his wound. "Everything NATO has available is being pulled back to defend Warsaw. Planes, men, tanks. It's all massing around the capital."

Edge grunted. "Okay. So if they're not pulling back to await an air strike they're either re-organizing for a new attack or –"

"Or we've been left for dead," Vince Waddingham said bleakly.

"Right," Edge admitted. "We have to face the possibility that help isn't coming and that we're going to have to find our own way back to the Army." He spoke simply, but behind his words he was seething. The Army had been mauled and humiliated by the Russians. The bridge crossing had been a diabolical disaster. Edge's pride was bruised. It was foolish, perhaps even naïve, but Edge was a proud soldier, raised with an undying faith in the American military's ability to overcome the sternest challenge. He wanted to strike back. He wanted to show the Russians that American Cavalry troopers were elite warriors who didn't know the meaning of defeat.

He wanted revenge.

"What will we do?" Kalina asked in a small voice. Her face was set and pale, but the fear showed in her eyes.

Edge shrugged. "The way I see it, we can either attempt to give the Russians the slip, or we have to surrender. Most of the wounded can't fight, and a lot of them aren't going to reach a field hospital," he said obliquely.

"I say we make another attempt to reach the woods," Vince Waddingham offered.

Captain Walker nodded agreement. "If we can hold out until dark…"

Edge shook his head. "The Russians aren't going to sit up on that ridge now the Squadron has disengaged," he said matter-of-factly. "Sooner or later they're going to send patrols to the bridge and along the riverbank."

"So you want to surrender?" Kalina frowned.

"No. I want to kill every one of the murdering Russian bastards," Edge's temper flared, revealing a glimpse of his inner thoughts. Then it faded again and his voice became neutral once more. "I enlisted to protect America from its enemies, and until someone tells me the war is over, I'm going to keep fighting because that's what soldiers do."

"Then we attempt an escape?" Waddingham asked. "How? To where?"

The afternoon began to turn cold. The sun was blood red behind drifting clouds of smoke. A small chill wind came hunting across the landscape, rustling the trees and abrading the surface of the river. Kalina shivered.

"You use the river," Edge spoke the idea that had been forming in the back of his mind since he had seen the bodies of the dead soldiers snagged amongst the bulrushes. "The current is flowing east. You take Captain Walker and you wade out into the middle of the river and let it carry you to safety. The Russians will think you're just more dead bodies. A mile from here the river bends. Once you reach that point, you'll be out of sight and out of danger."

"You kept saying 'you'. You meant 'we', right?" Waddingham asked.

Edge said nothing.

"What about the rest of the wounded?" Captain Walker's first concern was for the injured.

"Sir, most of them are not going to make it, and none of them would survive drifting downriver for several miles."

"So you want to leave them to die?"

"No. Their best chance of survival is surrender to the Russians. Maybe some of them will receive the medical help they need in time."

Walker grunted. Waddingham circled back to his original question, this time more forcefully.

"You kept saying 'you'…"

"That's right," Edge said. "You, Kalina, and the Captain. I'm not going."

"You're going to surrender with the wounded?"

"No, I'm going to get revenge," Edge vowed. "The Squadron might have disengaged from the battlefront but the fight isn't over. I'm going to get some payback for the men that died today."

Waddingham narrowed his eyes. "Then I'm coming with you."

"Vince, you can't," Edge made his tone reasonable. "You need to help the Captain to safety."

"Then I will help you," Kalina volunteered. Sweat had cut wet runnels through the dirt and mud that caked her cheeks.

"No. You're not trained, and Vince will need your help with the Captain and any other wounded men who want to attempt an escape."

Edge went from man to man, crawling through the mud to keep cover. The soldier who had taken a shrapnel wound to the groin was dead, his body already beginning to cool. The two other uninjured men volunteered to join the escape. The many injured meekly accepted that surrender was their only chance of survival. Edge told none of them about the plan in case Russian intelligence officers tortured them for details. When everything was prepared, Edge led the small group of escapees a hundred yards further along the bank.

"Wait for me downriver," he told Waddingham. "Find somewhere safe where you can hide, and leave a cairn of stones on the riverbank as a marker. If I haven't joined you by sunrise tomorrow, keep heading down river until you can cross to the far bank safely."

"I'll wait for you," Waddingham said stubbornly. He was unhappy and resentful. He gave Edge all the spare ammunition he could carry and then the soldiers stripped off their bulky body armor vests and kicked off their heavy boots. They buried the cache above the river's tideline. With Captain Walker supported between them, Waddingham and Kalina waded out into the river, followed by the two uninjured soldiers. They sank down into the blood-warm water until only their heads showed above the surface. Waddingham pushed off hard, propelling them out into the grip of the current.

Smoke lay like mist across the river's surface. Edge watched until the figures were just vague grey specks wreathed in haze, and then crept back to where the injured lay. He felt suddenly alone and vulnerable.

One of the wounded soldiers nursed a broken arm and leg, crushed under the tires of a Striker in the chaos of the battle. He lay propped against the bank of the river. He was groggy with pain, his face ashen. His eyes were deeply sunk into their sockets and shadowed by dark smudges the color of old bruises. Edge knelt beside the trooper.

"I need an hour," Edge said simply.

The soldier nodded. He was breathing in short shallow pants, his expression pain-wracked.

"When the time is up, start shouting that you surrender. The Russians won't be far away. The first thing they'll do is come down from the ridge to scout the crossing."

Again, the soldier nodded. He licked his lips. Edge gave the man his canteen of water and held it to his mouth while he drank greedily. He still carried his M4 slung across his lap. It was covered in mud.

"And keep your hands away from your weapon, soldier. The enemy's likely to be looking for any excuse…"

Edge moved fifty yards along the riverbank to where a knot of dense bushes grew. He squatted at the water's edge and slathered his face and hands in thick smears of mud, then plucked handfuls of long grass to stuff into the seams and openings of his uniform. He worked methodically, but the results were disappointing. He looked more like a straw scarecrow than a patch of meadow. But without a ghillie suit, it was the best he could do. He checked his weapon a final time then crept to the lip of the riverbank. Through the veil of bushy cover, he scanned the stretch of grass field ahead of him. He could see no sign of Russian troops, but he noticed the smoke was thinning, shredded by a stiffening afternoon breeze. He took a final deep breath and tensed himself – but the instant before he committed to going forward a shimmer of movement caught the corner of his eye. He turned his head and then swore bitterly and profusely beneath his breath.

Coming towards him along the riverbank, doubled over and covered in muddy slime, was Vince Waddingham.

"You stupid damn fool!"

Waddingham acted crestfallen. "Scout Team Leader Waddingham reporting for duty, Sergeant," he said formally.

"What the hell are you doing here?"

"Obeying orders, Sergeant."

"Orders? I told you to take care of the Captain. Whose damned orders?"

"Captain Walker's," Waddingham grinned.

"Captain Walker…?"

"Yes, Sergeant," Waddingham's mischievous smile widened. "He told me to come back and help you in your mission."

"Did he?" Edge asked with slow ominous menace.

"He did," Waddingham confirmed. "Even though I protested, Sergeant. Even though I insisted I should stay with him to ensure his safety because it was my duty as a good soldier."

"So you didn't prompt his decision?"

"No, Sergeant," Waddingham feigned shock at the suggestion, and fashioned his mud-streaked face into an expression of angelic innocence. "I'm just a humble Cavalry trooper. I go wherever a senior officer orders me."

Edge looked away to stop himself from smiling at Waddingham's delicate insolence. In truth he was relieved – although he could never admit it. He glared at Waddingham's broad grinning face a moment longer and then made his voice brusque. "I'm moving out in ten minutes. If you're not ready by then I'm going forward without you."

Waddingham was ready in nine, and together the two men crept to the lip of the riverbank. Slowly – very slowly – Edge and Waddingham snaked their way into the meadow of long grass, moving towards enemy lines.

It was time to take the war to the Russians.

Chapter 6:

They moved with agonizing restraint, hindered by their rudimentary camouflage and the fear that, from the crest of the ridge, a man with binoculars might easily see them. They crept across the field six inches at a time, careful not to disturb the grass, pulling themselves forward with their elbows, pushing off with their toes. Overhead the breeze stiffened and the smoke that had covered the battlefield since sunrise melted away.

The ground beneath them was hard. Edge suspected the area had once been a small field of crops; it was corrugated as though, years before, it had been under the plough. He kept his head down as he moved, losing track of time so that his entire world narrowed to the few feet directly ahead of him.

The two men lost contact. Edge was aware that Waddingham lay somewhere to his right but they never spoke, and he never sensed the other man's proximity. It was a solitary world of strain and sweat and tension. The only sound was his own hoarse breathing and the undulating rustle of the grass as it became fanned by the wind.

Twice in the first hour he slowly lifted his head to get his bearings, doing so each time with infinite caution, lifting his eyes just high enough to see the wall of trees on the far side of the field.

The sun on his back became hot and sweat ran in rivulets down his face. Then a sudden shot rang out, echoing against the sky. Edge froze and his heart slammed against the cage of his chest. He lay, unmoving for long seconds until he heard a sudden thin chorus of voices coming from somewhere behind him.

"We surrender! We surrender!"

Edge slowly let out the breath he was holding. It was the injured survivors on the riverbank. They had shot a round into the sky to attract the attention of the Russians. His time was up. An hour had passed.

He knew that within minutes a Russian patrol would come to investigate and until they had gathered up the prisoners all eyes would be on the stretch of river and on the field where he lay. He put his head down and remained still, using the time to regulate his breathing.

After a few minutes he felt a faint vibration through the ground and then heard the sudden high-revving noise of an engine. It sounded like a jeep. He knew the Russian Army had a number of off-road light utility vehicles. Most of them carried four men.

The vehicle braked to a halt and then followed the sound of running feet along the road that stopped suddenly. Edge imagined the soldiers with their weapons drawn, tense and wary of trouble as they clambered down the riverbank and stumbled upon the ragged handful of American soldiers.

For long minutes the silence overwhelmed him. He strained his ears for clues. An alarmed shout in Russian split the silence.

Edge couldn't understand the words but the tone was unmistakable. The voice was barking demands, but the replies were muffled. He heard one of the wounded men cry out, "But we surrender! We are injured and need medical aid!"

A second later the air filled with the violent slam of machine gun fire.

"Christ!" Edge listened, aghast. "They've executed them. The bastards. The filthy fucking bastards!"

He felt fury and rage rush over him. He felt his blood boil in his veins. A sudden violent madness overwhelmed his senses so that his instinct cried out for him to rise to his feet and fire on the murderers. It took every ounce of his restraint to lay still and resist the suicidal defiance. He clenched his fists until his fingernails dug deep bloody half-moons into his palm. He tightened his jaw until it ached.

After several minutes he heard the vehicle engine again. It sped away.

Edge waited another fifteen long minutes and then began to move. His eyes were still misted with red rage. He clawed himself forward, and the taste of his hatred was thick and bitter in the back of his throat, the flames fanned by the brutality of the callous murders.

He sensed the day passing and the gradual change of light. When he lifted his eyes slowly above the grass line for the final time he saw that it was late afternoon. Clouds hung low in the sky, casting the approaching sunset in dull eerie light. He crept on – and then suddenly a man's face emerged through the long grass.

He was dead.

He was one of the survivors who had joined the ill-fated charge across the open field. He lay on his back, his head twisted to the side. His mouth hung open, his lifeless eyes filled with an expression of bewilderment. There was dried dark blood on the man's cheek. Flies crawled into the cavity of his open mouth and across his eyeballs. He had been struck by a flurry of bullets. His chest had been pulped to a mush of blood and bone by multiple wounds.

Edge stared helplessly into the dead man's eyes, and made a silent, solemn vow. "You didn't die in vain," he promised.

He crawled past the body and began to move faster. He reached a patch of dull shadow and when he turned his eyes to the side he saw tall trees overhead. Edge kept crawling until the ground beneath him changed from corrugations of dry dirt to brown leaves and bark chips, and the afternoon light turned filtered and gloomy. He came up onto his haunches cautiously, his M4 on his hip. He had reached the fringe of the woods. He moved his eyes in a slow scan and saw Vince Waddingham concealed behind the cover of a tree, twenty yards to his right. Edge stayed motionless for sixty seconds and only when he was convinced the forest around him was empty did he finally move at a crouch to join Waddingham.

The Scout Team Leader's face was tight and snarling. "Did you hear it?" he hissed, his voice an accusing, infuriated whisper.

"Yeah," Edge answered.

"The fucking Russians murdered them, man. They put their guns to the heads of those poor injured bastards and blew their brains out."

"I know," Edge said darkly.

"We've gotta make them pay. We've gotta fight these bastards the way they're fighting us; no holds barred. That wasn't war. That was murder."

Edge nodded, and his eyes were black. "They will pay," he promised savagely.

*

They moved deeper into the woods. Edge lifted each boot with care, stepping lightly over the ground, watching each footfall to minimize the chance of noise. They moved in the shadows, avoiding areas where the trees were sparse, and they went forward at a crouch, weapons raised, pausing every few moments to stop, look and listen for danger.

Darkness came quickly to the woods. The night closed in around them. The scent of smoke still hung in the air, trapped beneath the canopy of trees.

"Vy chto-nibud' vidite?" a voice whispered out of the gloomy half-light. Edge and Waddingham froze.

"Net, nichego," the reply came from somewhere amongst the trees and Edge turned his waist slowly to hunt the voice, M4 at his shoulder, his eye along the weapon's sight. His finger curled and tensed over the trigger.

"Dvigaytes' dal'she na zapad."

Then Edge heard the soft sounds of leaves being scuffed by heavy boots and twigs breaking underfoot. A shape moved nearby in the dark, a shadow that seemed to float. He caught the movement out of the corner of his eye, and he tracked it without turning his head or daring to breath. He heard someone stifle a cough and then there was a loud clumsy stumble of jarring noise. The man cursed bitterly.

"Blyad'!"

"Vstavay, durak!" snapped the second voice, and they moved on, disappearing into the deep shadows until darkness hid them completely.

For a full five minutes Edge and Waddingham remained motionless, peering into the gloom while the sweat ran chill down their backs and alarm slid in their chests. Neither man had expected the Russians to be patrolling the woods. It was an additional danger they must account for.

"There could be more," Waddingham whispered when it was safe to talk.

Edge nodded.

They moved off again, trekking deeper into the woods. All of Edge's senses were heightened to compensate for the darkness. He could smell his own sweat and the cloying earthiness of decaying vegetation underfoot. He could feel the gentle breeze that came like a cool breath against his cheek. He could feel the clinging dampness of his sweat drenched clothes, and he could taste the rasping dryness in the back of his throat. He was breathing too quickly, the adrenaline rich in his veins.

The dense cover of trees around them began to thin and then stopped abruptly. Edge froze and lowered himself until he was laying prone. It was a stretch of cleared ground about fifteen feet wide that ran roughly east to west.

Waddingham dropped quietly down beside him.

"It's some kind of a disused fire trail through the woods," Edge whispered. "It must link up with the road across the bridge."

"Do you think it's patrolled?"

"Maybe."

"Do you think there's a sentry post nearby?"

"Probably."

Waddingham remained silent for just a moment. "I'll cross first."

He counted to ten, drew a deep breath and stepped out into the open space. The ground had been scored with the deeply-dug ruts of old tire tracks, long since overgrown with grass and covered by leaves. Waddingham moved silently and swiftly. He crossed the open space and dropped down into cover behind a shrub. Edge waited a few seconds and then followed.

No voices were raised in alarm. No gunfire ripped through the night. Edge and Waddingham pushed on.

The gradient began to change beneath Edge's feet, gradually at first and then more dramatically until he had to lean forward against it. They came across a section of woodland that had been scarred black by flames and shredded of foliage. Broken branches and clumps of leaves lay on the ground, still smoldering smoke. They circled the site and paused.

"I think we're nearing the eastern end of the ridgeline," Edge whispered. "It looks like the woods around here took a couple of stray shells from our batteries."

They continued to climb and the tension in them grew. Overhead the cloudbanks that had built along the horizon during the afternoon were now scudding across the moon so that the two scouts drifted in and out of silhouette. Finally they were forced to the ground to wait for more cloud cover. They were just below the crest of the ridge, beneath a sparse umbrella of leafy tree branches.

"We'll rest for five minutes," Edge muttered. He wiped his face on the sleeve of his uniform jacket.

"What do we do once we reach the ridgeline?" Waddingham asked. "Do we follow the spine west until we approach the road?"

"No," Edge shook his head. "That would bring us right down onto the saddle where the road crosses the rise. The Russians will be thick on the ground and they'll be entrenched. I want to get behind their lines." He thought for a moment and made up his mind. "We'll head down the opposite side of the hill and scout their position. Maybe we can pinpoint where their tanks are dug in, or maybe we can cause some mayhem and confusion."

"We're on a kill mission?"

Edge smiled thinly. It was a cruel twist of his lips, cold as a drawn steel blade and filled with savagery. "Yes."

*

When they were close to the crest, Edge crawled up to the skyline to peer down the far slope of the ridge.

And, through the palisade of tall dark tree trunks, saw a bright light.

He guessed the light was two hundred yards away, set in the middle of a tree-studded clearing. Waddingham crept forward until he was laying prone at Edge's elbow.

"What the fuck are they doing?" he asked when he saw the glare of white light. "Are they searching for us?"

"They don't know we exist."

"Then what are they doing?"

Edge shrugged. "Let's go and find out. We crawl from here."

They slithered down the slope like snakes, creeping through the dense blanket of leafy ground cover that lay strewn across the forest floor. They moved with painstaking caution until they reached the foot of the hill. Still within the fringe of trees, they stared out across a clearing of grassy ground that was sprinkled with dark clumped bushes.

Four Russian vehicles were parked in a crude circle beside a dirt trail, starkly silhouetted by the bright light. Two of the vehicles looked like light-utility Russian jeep variants. One of them was a canvas-covered cargo truck. But it was the fourth vehicle that drew all of Edge's attention. It looked like an armored personnel carrier without a turret; an eight-wheeled elongated steel hull on tires. The rear engine hatch of the vehicle was open and Edge saw that the light was a small arc lamp attached to an upright post, powered by a generator which was surrounded by sandbags to muffle the noise.

"It's the Russian command post," Edge's voice was wolfish. He studied the four vehicles and then turned his attention to the perimeter of the clearing. The dirt trail ran west, he presumed to link up with the road. He guessed the clearing was another old farm field that had once hosted crops. Now the ground was overgrown by weeds and wild bushes. There was a sparse sprinkle of trees on the far side of the clearing that would have offered some cover, but Edge knew he would have no chance of circling the field before daylight. He turned his attention back to the squat eight-wheeled armored vehicle just in time to see a flicker of movement and a soft clink of noise. He tensed, then saw the silhouette of a soldier on his knees.

"Looks like they have engine trouble," Waddingham said. "That's why the arc light is set up. They're trying to fix the issue."

Edge made a quick calculation. They were perhaps a hundred yards away from the vehicles. It was not an impossible shot with the M4, but the darkness made the task more difficult. But to creep within range of certain kills would mean crawling through another field of long grass – and every second would be a moment of high risk.

"We're moving in," he decided, despite the danger. "I'm going to get close enough to take a shot. If that is a command vehicle, it means there must be a high-ranking officer somewhere nearby. I'm going to lay up in the field and wait for my chance. I want you to circle to the west and find an ambush point," he indicated the dirt trail that ran towards the road. "Once I open fire, anyone and everyone within earshot is going to come running. Take out as many as you can. We'll rendezvous back on the opposite side of the ridge where we intersected the fire trail."

Waddingham hesitated as though he wanted to ask questions, then decided simply to follow the plan. He nodded agreement.

Edge had a final word of warning. "If I'm not back at the rendezvous point by three in the morning, move on without me. Link up with Kalina and the Captain, and make your way back to the Squadron."

*

Major Konstantin Bondarchuk lit another cigarette and waited impatiently for the radio operator to relay his message. It was cramped inside the Russian R-145BM mobile command vehicle, with most of the available space dedicated to banks of radio communication equipment and a folding map table. Bondarchuk was a big bear of a man with a shock of white hair. He felt trapped in a steel coffin. All the hatches were open but still the air inside the vehicle was ripe with the stench of sweat and smoke.

He sat drumming his fingers on the tabletop through thirty long seconds of static and then snarled at the radio man.

"Damn it! Let me know when you send the message and have a reply from Shock Army Command."

He clambered out of the vehicle through a wide hatch in the hull and growled at the mechanic working on the engine.

"Well?"

"No success yet, Major," the enlisted recruit said fretfully. "I suspect it might be a problem with the fuel lines."

"Fix it!" Bondarchuk snapped. Despite the day's triumph against the American armored Stryker column he was in a foul mood. He had lost sixty-three men in the fighting, mainly to American canister and HEAT shells, with a further twenty-one men wounded. If the Americans returned in the morning, he would have less than a hundred soldiers left of his two-Company command to repel the next assault… and two T-90 tanks. They were the muscle of his defense; the iron fists that had smashed the American attack and tore it to pieces. The tanks were positioned hull down on either side of the road as it rose up through the saddle of the ridge, carefully concealed and well protected. Bondarchuk had chosen the sites personally.

He crushed the cigarette out beneath his boot and strode to the nearest of the two Iveco LMV's. Three junior officers were huddled around the 4WD vehicle, talking animatedly. They snapped to attention when the Major's hulking frame emerged into the glaring light.

"Casualty report?" Bondarchuk demanded.

"Three more of the men who were injured in today's fighting have since died, Major," a pale-faced Lieutenant stammered.

Bondarchuk grunted. Injured or dead – it mattered little to him. If the wounded men could not fight tomorrow, they might as well be dead, he reasoned. Any man who could not raise a weapon was a useless drain on resources.

"And the Americans?"

"We're waiting for satellite images, Major," A Captain answered. "But our best intelligence estimate suggests they have retreated to the west."

Bondarchuk shook his great shaggy head and eyed the officer contemptuously. "They might have withdrawn, but retreat? No," he spoke to the officer the way a parent speaks to a small, slow-witted child. "Mark my words. They will be back, and when they return we must be ready to give them another bloody nose."

*

Edge lay in the tall grass in the middle of the open field, a scant thirty yards from the Russian armored command vehicle. He was lathered in sweat, every nerve drawn tight. His heart thumped so loudly in his chest that he was sure the knot of Russian soldiers backlit by the arc lamp must surely hear him. He felt horribly exposed and vulnerable. He knew he would have just one fleeting opportunity for revenge before all hell broke loose.

He took careful aim, drew a breath and began to exhale as he squeezed the trigger. The M4 roared in his hands.

The hail of close-range gunfire cut down the four Russian officers and dashed their blood against the side of the Iveco, painting the vehicle in ghastly lurid splatters.

The tall Major was the first to die. He clutched at his stomach, his expression startled. Blood seeped from between his fingers and then he slowly fell forward like a toppled tree.

The knot of three junior officers were cut down in the swathe of gunfire. The impact flung them back against the vehicle and the flaming roar of the M4 drowned out their agonized cries as they died. One of the men was struck in the throat as he turned towards the gunfire. His mouth sagged open and a gush of blood fountained down the front of his tunic. He was dead before he hit the dirt.

Fighting his instinct to flee, Edge pounced to his feet and dashed forward. He crouched over the four Russian bodies for several seconds, and when he came to his feet again, he had grenades in his hands. He dropped one down through the open hatch of the command vehicle and lobbed the second into the open door of an Iveco. The vehicles erupted in a great booming thunder of fire and smoke. He shot the startled mechanic in the chest and then killed two more Russians who came running out of the shadows. They might have been mechanics or perhaps drivers; Edge had no way of telling. He cut them down with a burst of chattering gunfire.

Edge turned and fled. He was halfway back to the safety of the tree line before Vince Waddingham suddenly opened fire. The sound of the M4 was like the noise of a great sheet of canvas being torn apart. Edge saw a flickering tongue of flame from the corner of his eye about a hundred yards to the west. Edge ran on, lifting his legs high and pumping his arms to drive himself through the long grass until, at last, the dark fringe of woods enveloped him. He crashed through the undergrowth and in his haste he cannoned off a tree trunk then trapped his foot in a gnarled twist of roots. He bounced to his feet and put himself to the hilly slope. The sound of two more far-away explosions that echoed across the night told him Vince Waddingham was still killing Russians.

*

"Not yet," Captain Walker said. His voice was weak but his tone stubborn. "We'll wait until noon. By then we will know for sure."

Kalina knelt over the Captain and shook her head, but she did not protest. Walker's face was pale, his lips bloodless. His eyes had sunk into their sockets and the flesh across his cheeks was drawn so tightly that he looked gaunt and feverish. He lay stretched out beside the riverbank, beneath the branches of a shady tree. Kalina had stripped him to the waist and used his jacket as a makeshift pillow. The flesh around the bullet hole in the Captain's shoulder was livid red and swollen – but no longer bleeding.

They had heard the far-off chatter of gunfire during the night and the echo of several explosions. Since then, the two soldiers who accompanied them had stood a constant vigil by the riverbank. Now the sun was rising on a new day.

"If you do not soon get medical attention you will die," Kalina said.

"A few more hours won't make a difference," Captain Walker countered and then compromised when he saw the look on the Polish woman's face. She had a fiery temper and little respect for rank. "Two more hours," he bargained. "If Edge and Waddingham haven't returned by then, we'll make our way back to the Squadron."

She nodded curt agreement and got to her feet. They hadn't eaten since the previous day and they were down to their last canteen of water. Kalina went to the river and stared west. The sun was rising from over her shoulder, painting the smooth water's surface with reflected shades of gold and copper, and casting the land in long morning shadow. They were, all of them, covered from head to toe in filth and grime and mud. She crouched ankle deep in the water and saw her own reflection mirrored. The face that stared back was haggard with exhaustion and fatigue. She scooped up a handful of water and began to wash the mud from her face so that it was several seconds before she became aware of the sudden electricity of excitement that charged the atmosphere. She rose to her feet and followed the outstretched pointing arm of one of the soldiers. He was staring up river where two dark blobs of shape bobbed and dipped.

Edge and Waddingham had found them.

The two men had been carried almost six miles downstream. As the current swept them around the river's bend, they had seen small figures by the water's edge in the distance. Edge felt a rush of relief and began kicking out towards the bank. Kalina waded out into the water to meet them, keeping her voice quiet.

"You can stand up," she said. "The water is shallow."

Edge planted his feet in the muddy riverbed and stood. The water in the middle of the river only reached to his waist. He and Waddingham waded ashore, streaming mud and slime. They collapsed in the long grass, their chests heaving, their arms aching.

They lay like that for several minutes, overcome with the heavy weight of their fatigue. Then Edge sat up with a sudden start.

"The river," he said as the realization dawned on him. "Christ! You've discovered a natural fording point. Do you realize what this means?"

Suddenly the crushing exhaustion lifted from him like a cast off cloak, and he was eager to be on his way. The two soldiers fashioned a crude stretcher for the Captain using long tree branches and tied tunic jackets. Ten minutes later they waded across the Sypitki and onto the far bank.

Edge was in a hurry to rejoin the Cavalry.

The battle to win the bridge was not over.

Chapter 7:

Several of the Strykers had flat tires. Many were scarred, dented and blood-splattered, their steel hulls gouged by ricocheting machine gun fire. The side of one vehicle had been scorched black from its proximity to a mortar blast and one of its wheels was buckled.

The forest was a hive of subdued activity; soldiers bustled between maintenance and repair tasks with bleak, sullen expressions. Men growled irritably at each other under a black pall of gloom that hung over the forest, thick as smoke.

Edge stood under the shade of a tree and watched a vehicle's crew replenish the autoloader of an M1128 with fresh shrapnel canisters and HEAT rounds. He felt exhausted; the kind of bone-weary fatigue that not even a shower and a meal were able to erase.

"HEAT, carousel one," the vehicle's driver carried a round from a parked M977 HEMTT ammo truck and loaded it through the open rear doors of the Stryker.

"HEAT, carousel one," the vehicle's gunner, stationed inside the vehicle, repeated the information as he inputted the data into the vehicle's fire control computer.

"Cannister, carousel two," the driver leaned through the open doors with another round. As he straightened, he saw Edge watching him. The Stryker's driver was a fresh-faced young man with haunted eyes behind steel-rimmed glasses. In the background an M1078 LMTV food truck bounced and revved loudly along a makeshift dirt trail, escorted by a Humvee and a Stryker.

"Was it your first time in action?" Edge asked quietly.

The young man nodded. His face was deathly pale.

"It gets better," Edge reassured him. It sounded unconvincing, even to Edge, and the young trooper did not reply. He just pushed his glasses up onto the bridge of his nose with his fingertip and strode back to the ammunition truck for another shrapnel canister. Edge turned away to watch the arrival of a fuel truck.

A voice called out to him, loud and insistent, and a Lieutenant, dressed in a rumpled sweat-stained uniform, beckoned to Edge. "Sergeant?"

"Yes, sir."

"Colonel Sutcliffe will meet you now in the TOC." The Lieutenant tried to soften the order with an engaging smile. He looked Edge up and down and grimaced as though his appearance was cringeworthy. "Do you want to change, or wash?"

Edge tugged at the sleeves of his OCP top. "I have washed."

The Lieutenant's smile did not falter. "Follow me. We don't want to keep the Colonel waiting any longer than necessary."

They strode through the press of bustling activity, weaving between parked vehicles, stepping around mechanics and boxes of machine gun ammunition. The Lieutenant kept glancing over his shoulder to be sure Edge was on his heel. As they walked, he filled Edge in on the events following the decision to withdraw the Squadron from the bridge.

"The Colonel was struck by shrapnel when the Su-25 attacked the column. Luckily it was only a flesh wound. The medics have patched him up but he's like a bear with a sore head," the Lieutenant warned. "You might need a whip and a chair…"

"Have we called for air support, sir?" Edge kept pace with the Lieutenant.

"Yes, but it's not going to happen. Every air asset is being centered on the impending defense of Warsaw. I'm afraid we're on our own."

They reached the clearing where the TOC stood. A Humvee was parked outside the main tent. A trooper knelt washing blood from the interior with a bucket of water and a brush. The Lieutenant stopped and turned back to Edge, pointing a warning with his finger. "I don't know why, or what you've done, Sergeant, but the Polish Major wants your head served on a platter. He's convinced you are to blame for the failed attack."

"Me?" Edge snarled.

The Lieutenant nodded. "He's been calling for your court-martial."

An armed sentry stood outside the tent. He stepped aside as Edge approached. The Lieutenant gave him a last pitying look. "Good luck. You're going to need it."

Edge ducked under the flap of the tent to find himself face-to-face with Major Nowakowski. The Polish officer's lips were curled into a snarl of distain. He glared at Edge, his eyes blazing.

"Damn you! Your faulty scouting report of the terrain around the bridge has cost over a hundred lives and lead to the destruction of several armored vehicles. I am going to see that you pay for your dereliction of duty. I am going to see you broken, Sergeant Edge. Broken and driven from the Army!" Nowakowski's face was a savage mask of anger. The NATO diplomat tried to tactfully intervene, plucking at the Polish Major's elbow to draw him away. Nowakowski shook the tall German man's hands off. "Your cowardice is unworthy of your nation's fine military tradition – and it's unworthy of my brave men and women who lost their lives due to your negligence!"

Edge kept his composure, drawing his face rigid until the Squadron's XO came forward from the far end of the tent. He held a copy of Edge's report in his hand. Ignoring Nowakowski, the Executive Officer gestured for Edge to follow him. The blustering red-faced Polish Major followed unbidden, yapping at Edge's heels until the knot of aides in the corner of the tent parted.

Colonel Sutcliffe sat slumped in a chair, favoring his injured side. His chest had been swathed in fresh bandages. Edge stood to attention and saluted. Sutcliffe's expression was unreadable.

"Well, what do you have to say for yourself?" the Colonel asked. He lifted a copy of the hasty report Edge had written on his return from the river and looked at it.

"There is a fordable crossing, sir. It's about six clicks east of the bridge."

The Colonel flipped through the pages until he found Edge's map. He narrowed his eyes, his expression calculating as he studied the terrain. Then he closed the file and sighed heavily. "You say you took out the Russian command element?"

"Yes, sir."

"On your own?"

"No, sir. Scout Team Leader, Sergeant Waddingham, was with me."

The Colonel and his XO exchanged a pointed glance. "Do you know who you killed?"

"A Russian Major, a Captain and two Lieutenant's, sir. I also destroyed their command vehicle and a 4WD with grenades."

"Rubbish!" Major Nowakowski interrupted. His voice thrust like a cold steel blade. He too had read Edge's report. Now he pushed his way into the knot of men around the Colonel and his voice was loud with oily triumph. "If your report is accurate, Sergeant, then how could you possibly know the ranks of the men you claim to have shot? You said yourself that the action took place in the dark hours of early morning, and that the only light came from an arc lamp. You expect us to believe you could identify the ranks of the men you claim to have killed? They could have been cooks, or medical staff!"

There was a long chill silence. The air crackled with the challenge. Without saying a word Edge reached into the pocket of his pants and threw a handful of epaulettes onto a table. There were four strips of camouflaged cloth, each one decorated with Russian ranking pips. The Squadron XO picked up one of the epaulettes. It was a patch of camouflaged fabric inset with a large metallic star.

"After I killed the four officers, I went forward and took their epaulettes," Edge explained. His voice was tight with forced restraint so that he seemed to speak through clenched teeth.

Colonel Sutcliffe let his gaze drift to the stunned expression on the Polish Officer's face.

"Well, Major Nowakowski?" the Colonel asked with arch politeness. "Do you have any more questions for Sergeant Edge?"

The Polish Major flushed crimson with indignation. He blustered for a moment and then lapsed into simmering silence. He was pale with anger. Sutcliffe gave the man a cold contemptuous stare and then dismissed him from his thoughts. He turned his attention back to Edge and became brisk and business-like.

"You found the ford by accident?"

"I didn't discover it, sir," Edge said. "Kalina Nowakowski from the Polish Territorial Defense Force and survivors under the command of Captain Walker found the site. They escaped the Russians by drifting downriver while Sergeant Waddingham and I went inland to scout the enemy's defenses."

Sutcliffe looked thoughtful. His XO leaned close and muttered a comment in the Colonel's ear. Sutcliffe nodded, then regarded Edge speculatively. "And what do you think our next move should be, Sergeant?"

Edge seemed surprised that he was asked, and equally surprised that the question required an answer. He had considered the military options from every angle during the trek from the river to rejoin the Squadron. There was only one clear solution.

"We outflank the bastards," he said and then covered his blunt outburst with a belated, " – sir." Sutcliffe smiled thinly. Edge went on. "We hit them immediately while they are disorganized and without leadership, Colonel, and we slaughter them."

Sutcliffe nodded. He looked impossibly tired. He was helped to his feet by an aide and moved to a map affixed to a whiteboard. He peered at the terrain for a long moment. The tent remained silent, broken only by the distant sound of revving engines. It struck Edge that the Colonel was hesitating. Sutcliffe turned back to him.

"We lost over a dozen Strykers today trying to take the bridge, as well as two Mortar Carriers. More than a hundred men were killed in the assault, and many more died when the Russian ground-attack aircraft pounced," he lapsed into a long moment of reflective silence and then straightened suddenly as though waking from a bleak nightmare. "There are some amongst NATO Command who believe we should withdraw – pull back to Warsaw and abandon the attack against the flank of the Russian spearhead." Sutcliffe didn't need to glance in the direction of the tall German diplomat for Edge to understand that politics were in play. "But I'm not prepared to accept that the young men and women who died on the battlefield today gave their lives for nothing. It's not the Cavalry way."

Edge nodded.

The Colonel's eyes flicked to Nowakowski.

"Major?"

"Colonel Sutcliffe?"

"We're attacking the bridge again tonight."

The Polish Major said nothing. He was still simmering with affront, still stinging from insult. He continued to glower at Edge in hateful silence.

The Colonel turned away from the map. He seemed filled with renewed grim resolve as he addressed the rest of the room. "Gentlemen, spread the word. We'll reconvene in an hour from now for a briefing."

Sutcliffe's final words were for Edge. "Be back here in an hour. Tonight's attack is based on your intelligence, so I want you on hand to share everything you saw. And bring Sergeant Waddingham with you."

*

Edge spent the hour between leaving and returning to the TOC sitting with Waddingham under the shade of a tree. The conversation was desultory. A medic interrupted their companionable peace to inform Edge that Captain Walker was being evacuated. Then Kalina Nowakowski found the two men.

She came through the woods following a tire-worn trail from the Polish camp. She had washed and changed her uniform. She regarded Edge with cool professional detachment, but her voice was surprisingly soft.

"I heard what happened," she said, indicating the distant shape of the TOC with a jerk of her head. "It's the second time you have embarrassed my father."

Edge said nothing. Kalina squatted down in the grass and looked away for a moment as if searching for words. She smiled thinly. "My father has ambitions of political power in Poland," she explained. "He thinks he is the nation's next Tadeusz Kosciuszko."

Edge shrugged. His tone turned surly. "Never heard of him."

"He was a famous Polish military engineer, statesman and military leader who became a national hero two hundred years ago. My father aspires to political power and sees his route to leadership through bold military victories. This war, for him, is an opportunity to make a reputation."

"Your father is nothing but a strutting peacock," Edge said with icy belligerence. "He likes to play at being a great general, but war is no place for amateurs. Your father is going to get a lot of soldiers killed – and you might be one of them."

"He's entitled –" she began the mild reproof.

"Entitled? He's not even skilled enough to rank as a Lieutenant," Edge's voice brimmed with contempt. "And I'll be damned if I'll stand by and take the blame for his failings."

Kalina's cheeks flushed red. She rose slowly to her feet. "I didn't come here to argue with you. I came to warn you. My father is a dangerous, vindictive and ambitious man. He won't let anyone stand between his path to glory – not even an American Sergeant. You must watch your back. He will look for revenge."

*

Edge stormed out of the TOC tent in a simmering, fiery mood; a volcano of rage on the brink of eruption. Sergeant Waddingham recognized the signs and knew well enough that Edge needed to vent his frustration, so like a lion tamer thrusting his head into the jaws of a savage beast, he asked with bemused mildness, "What do you think of the plan?"

Edge snarled but did not speak or slow his pace. He just stormed off through the woods towards the four vehicles of 2nd Platoon. It was late afternoon, yet the warmth of the day remained trapped beneath the forest canopy, tainting the languid air with the odors of sweat and fuel fumes.

"I'm looking forward to working with the Polish troops," Waddingham enthused, goading Edge into a reaction. "They're going to be right in the thick of the fighting tonight."

Edge's step faltered and for a moment it seemed he might turn and snap a comment. But instead he stiffened with restraint and marched on. Waddingham trailed in his shadow.

"Do you think Major Nowakowski will personally lead the attack? It would certainly make me feel more confident knowing his vast military experience and undoubted leadership qualities were guiding us forward when we engage the Russians," Vince Waddingham grinned.

That was it.

Edge spun on his heel, spitting venom. His eyes blazed with malevolence. "Fucking Nowakowski is a useless fuckin' show-pony. The damned fool is likely to get us killed!"

"Do you think?" Waddingham taunted him.

"Yes, I fuckin' do!" Edge snapped. "Christ! The whole plan depends on that bastard. It's madness. Utter madness."

Waddingham shrugged and his tone sobered. "The river crossing…"

The Sypitki.

The plan the Colonel outlined for the night attack called for the column of Polish Wolverines to ford the river and then sweep west to crash upon the Russian flank, supported by three M1128 MGS's loaded with sabot rounds and guided by Edge's scout Platoon. To ensure surprise the 1ˢᵗ Squadron would first mount a feint attack on the bridge. The Polish column had grudgingly been given the critical outflanking role because the Wolverines were 'amphibious'. The Strykers were not.

"Nowakowski's a bastard," Edge said savagely. "And I don't trust him."

Waddingham stared off into the distance. In truth he shared Edge's misgivings. Major Nowakowski's hunger for glory and his complete lack of combat experience might turn the attack into an abject disaster – and there was nothing anyone could do to prevent it.

He was about to say more when he saw the Squadron's Command Sergeant Major striding towards them. The CSM was the senior enlisted NCO, and Colonel Sutcliffe's right-hand man. He was a big, burly veteran with a buzz-cut of grey spikes and a weather-worn face, creased as a city roadmap.

"You seem pissed," CSM Perryman gruffed. He looked Edge up and down, his gaze challenging.

"I'm not fuckin' happy," Edge admitted.

Perryman shrugged. "No one is, including the Colonel."

Edge frowned. "The plan was his."

"No. The plan was a diplomatic deal. NATO had to be appeased."

"NATO? You mean this cluster fuck is all because of politics?"

"Of course," Perryman said. "But that doesn't mean the Colonel wants you getting caught up in Nowakowski's grand plan for glory. You're to guide the Wolverines through the woods to the ambush point and nothing more. There'll be no mad heroics, understand?"

Edge stared at the CSM and got a nod for confirmation. Clearly the Colonel was just as unhappy with the arrangements as Edge.

Edge understood. The Polish Major was pushing his own ambitious agenda for glory and using the fragile NATO alliance as a bargaining tool to make a name for himself.

Edge let his thoughts drift. In his imagination he saw the forest on the far side of the river that linked the shallow crossing point to the flank of the Russian's dug in defending the road. He saw his Strykers moving forward and the Wolverines in their wake, creeping closer to the enemy as the minutes prior to attack ticked down. Then he saw the Polish Major waving his Wolverines forward impulsively, hell-bent on glory and triumph. In his mind he saw the Russians on the edge of the woods turn with their RPG's and the sudden chaos as the Wolverines ran impetuously into the hail of missiles. The forest would erupt in fireballs and smoke and the element of surprise would be lost, along with any hope of capturing the bridge…

"What if Nowakowski leads his troops on mad charge for glory?"

"Let him," Perryman said bluntly.

"And if I'm ordered to support his stupidity?"

"Ignore him," Perryman said. "You don't take orders from Major Nowakowski. You've been attached to his column to guide him to the enemy. You take your orders from Colonel Sutcliffe – and so do the MGS's."

*

Edge assembled the troopers of 2nd Platoon around him and explained their role in the upcoming attack. The men listened in stony silence. Then it was time for the pre-battle rituals. Soldiers stripped down their weapons and re-assembled them, re-loaded magazines, and attended obsessively to the myriad of small details that might make the difference between life and death in a battle. Men who carried M9 bayonets sharpened the lengths of steel to a razor's edge and tested the blades by shaving hair from their forearms.

Then all four of the vehicles were given the same dedicated attention; engines were tuned, tire pressures checked, spare magazines for the 50cal machine guns loaded aboard and everything loose tied down or tightened. Finally the fuel tanks were brimmed full.

An hour before sunset, the four Strykers moved out. Keeping their speed low to avoid tell-tale rooster-tails of dust across the skyline, they took a wide swinging route to the river, hooking well to the east and then following the banks of the Sypitki until they reached the crossing point.

The vehicles parked well away from the riverbank behind a dense grove of trees. Every man was on alert. The rear doors of Edge's Stryker swung open. Waddingham and the three other members of his scout team dismounted.

Edge led the scouts to the riverbank, creeping cautiously as the night closed in. The sun sat low in the sky and a chill breeze came hunting across the landscape, whipping through the long grass and rustling the leaves in the trees.

When they reached the bank of the Sypitki they found their own trail of scuffed footprints by the water's edge, left behind when they had emerged from the river only a dozen hours earlier.

Edge and Waddingham crouched close to the water. Nightfall came crashing down around them. The trees on the far side of the river turned to dark silhouettes and the first stars appeared in the sky. The rim of the world was lit by the pale glow of last light.

"Once you're across the river, I want you to take your men five hundred yards west, towards the Russian positions," Edge spoke quietly. "Set up a perimeter and stay in contact." He checked his watch. The 1st Squadron were scheduled to commence their feint attack on the bridge at 2015 hours, and the column of Polish Wolverines were due to reach the river crossing an hour after nightfall to ensure their arrival went undetected. "If it's all clear in thirty minutes, I'll bring the two 'A' section Strykers across as support. Hal Calhoun will remain with the last two Platoon vehicles on this side of the river to guide the Polish column across. Once everyone is over the river safely, well push north until we intersect the fire trail that you and I discovered last night. That will be the assembly point."

Waddingham nodded. He had smeared his face in camouflage paint. He motioned his squad forward and the scouts waded waist-deep into the black burbling current of the river. Waddingham and Edge made a final time hack. "I'll see you on the other side in half an hour."

*

All the light had been bled from the western sky and now the night was dark. Edge glanced at his watch. Waddingham and his scout team had been gone for fifteen minutes. Hal Calhoun sidled up to him from out of the shadows and thrust a tin mug of coffee into Edge's hands. He accepted it gratefully and turned to stare across the horizon for any sign of the approaching Polish Wolverines.

Nothing.

It was too early to fret. The column was not expected for another forty-five minutes… and yet Edge felt a faint twinge of apprehension. He shivered slightly and walked a slow path between the parked Strykers with Calhoun at his side. The troopers were waiting idly. Some read dog-eared paperbacks. Others penned quick notes to loved-ones back home. One of the scouts dozed fitfully. Every man had his own personal way of dealing with the anxiety before combat.

Edge left the tree-sheltered grove and walked down to the river's edge. A sentry heard him coming. The man was laying prone in the tall grass by the riverbank.

"Anything?"

The scout shook his head.

The night was ominously quiet as though the world held its breath, anticipating the dreadful horror that would follow.

Edge stayed by the riverbank for several minutes, his ears straining for any sound that might presage danger. Fish splashed in the water and from somewhere in the distance an owl hooted and the night sky filled with the beat of huge wings.

Finally it was time. He cast the dregs from his coffee mug into the grass and walked briskly back to the waiting Strykers. "Mount up."

Engines rumbled to life, belching black exhaust into the night. Edge drew Calhoun aside.

"The Poles should be here within thirty minutes. Bring them straight across the river. We have to be in position to launch the attack when the distraction around the bridge kicks off, so keep 'em moving."

Hal Calhoun smiled. "You're talkin' to a Texan. Herding ornery cattle is in my blood."

The two 'A' section Strykers moved down to the riverbank with Edge's vehicle in the lead. The driver nosed the vehicle into the water, moving at slow speed and low revs, pushing a bow-wave. The river rose to the top of the huge tires and sprayed the air with rain-like mist. The second Stryker followed close behind, churning the loose muddy riverbed. Both vehicles emerged onto the far bank, streaming water, their chunky tire treads scrabbling for purchase.

Edge stood upright in the command hatch, issuing orders in a subdued voice while the driver sat hunched over his controls, steering through his DVE. The AN/VAS-5 Driver Vision Enhancer was a passive thermal imaging system designed for use in darkness or periods of degraded visibility during combat, but even with the technological assistance, stealth proved impossible. The forest on the fringe of the river was dense, the ground rocky and uneven. Every engine rev and every felled sapling in their path made Edge cringe.

Finally Vince Waddingham loomed out of the darkness, glowing green in Edge's night-vision goggles. He waved the vehicle to a halt and the silence of the night slammed down around them.

Edge dismounted from the Stryker and went forward. Waddingham leaned close to his ear and indicated the positions of his scout team. "We're all clear. No sign of the enemy."

Edge checked his watch.

The scouts moved another hundred yards deeper into the woods and Edge positioned the Strykers to overwatch their advance and protect the river crossing. Through the canopy of leaves the night sky filled with stars and the forest came alive with insects. It would still be a few minutes, Edge decided, before the rumble of the arriving Wolverines would drown out the silence. He walked the perimeter, moving between the scouts, and then came back to where Waddingham crouched.

The two men did not speak. They both knew the mission, and both understood the risks that came with the work. Edge's stomach grumbled, reminding him that he hadn't eaten in hours. He checked his watch and grunted.

"It's time."

He listened hard into the distance, expecting to hear the approaching Polish armored vehicles. The night was unsettlingly quiet. Edge felt the first premonition of trouble slide in his chest. He went back to the Stryker, frowning.

"White Two, White One," Edge called on the Platoon net. "Are the Polish Wolverines in position?"

"One, this is Two," Hal Calhoun replied. "Negative. They have not arrived. Repeat. They have not arrived – and we've had no word from HQ about the cause of the delay."

"Christ!" Edge cut comms in a sudden white-hot fit of fury.

He went forward to Waddingham, seething with anger. He swore bitterly. "The fucking Poles haven't arrived! No one knows where they are!"

"You're shitting me," Waddingham snapped his head round.

It took all of Edge's restraint to prevent himself from raising his voice to a shout. "They should have been here ten minutes ago."

"So what do we do?"

"We wait," Edge fumed. "And we hope the fucking Poles turn up in the next few minutes, because otherwise the men attacking the bridge are going to get slaughtered for no reason. No damn reason at all."

It was a somber thought. The Strykers of 1st Squadron would be massing around the bridge, the MGS's taking up overwatch positions behind cover and preparing to fire. The main column would be drawn up on the road with their engines idling, waiting for the 'Go!' order. The troopers in the rear of each vehicle would be tense and anxious. Other infantry would be dismounted, crawling through the long grass to the riverbank, from where they could lay down suppressing fire. Once the Russian mortars began counter-fire, those troops would be horribly exposed. And every minute the feint attack continued, more men would die needlessly…

"It don't seem right," Waddingham said bitterly. "I mean this is their country. We're fighting in Poland to defend their capital, their towns and their farms from a Russian invasion… and their own military can't be bothered turning up on time for the battle?"

"It's not the Polish troops. It's that arrogant bastard, Nowakowski," Edge's voice was a vengeful, savage snarl. "And I swear to God, when this is all over, I'm going to make him pay."

Chapter 8:

The sudden percussive cough of a far-away explosion, followed soon after by another, startled Edge and brought him to sudden anxious alert. Three seconds later the night was lit by a dazzling white orb of light that hung in the sky, suspended on a trickling tail of smoke. A moment afterwards the second light flared, bright as the sun.

"Illumination rounds," Waddingham said.

Edge glared at his watch, sick with dread. "They've started the attack on the bridge too early."

"They're not our flares," Waddingham said with foreboding. "They're Russian."

"Oh, Christ!" Edge groaned.

It was a nightmare.

The Russians had somehow been alerted to the American armored column's advance and had opened fire. In a single second of misfortune, the initiative had been lost. Now the killing would begin.

The sky became criss-crossed with arcs of flaring light and the smoke trails of shells passing in the sky. The horizon glowed orange, pulsing with the flashing bloom of each new explosion. The air seemed to quiver with the roll and punch of every salvo. The stars became blotted out by a thick blanket of smoke that was twitched and torn by new salvos that glowed red inside the clouds.

Edge bounced to his feet and sprinted back to the Stryker. There was no longer any need for stealth. Now speed was all that mattered. He snatched up the radio and his voice was urgent.

"White Two, White One. Have the Polish Wolverines arrived?"

There was a delay before Calhoun's voice filled the static hiss. "One, this is Two. Negative. Still no sign of the column."

"Fuck!" Edge swore. He clawed his fingers through his hair, fuming with impotent frustration. "Two, this is One. I want you to go and find the bastards. Understand? Leave the other Stryker by the riverbank in case they turn up."

"One, Two. Roger."

Edge slammed the radio into its cradle and sprinted back through the screen of woods.

"What's happening?" Waddingham muttered.

Edge crouched down and growled. "Still no sign of the Polish." He could see Waddingham's face in the dull glowing light but behind his camouflage paint it was too dark to read his expression. "I sent Calhoun out into the night to look for the bastards."

From the west the sounds of fighting intensified. What had started as a flurry of flares and mortar shells had turned into the savage full-throated roar of battle.

*

For a brief gut-churning, heart-stopping moment the Cavalry troopers around the bridge were caught in the bright glare of Russian illumination rounds – picked out in stark relief against the pitch black of the night.

Then their world turned to hell.

The Russians had the range to the bridge already zeroed in. They didn't need to know exactly where the Americans were. They only needed to know they were making another attempt to seize the bridge. Mortar shells began to fall like rain, churning the ground to a slurry of muddy furrows and spewing deadly shrapnel. Inevitably men on the road and along the riverbank began to fall. Some were killed outright, shredded to pieces by the booming barrage of explosions. Others were scythed down and fell into the long grass clutching at gruesome wounds. Cries of pain and agony filled the space between each fresh explosion, becoming shrill with panic and desperation. Freshly spilled blood spattered the blacktop and soaked the fields.

The MGS's behind low cover to the east of the bridge returned fire, their muzzle flares lighting up the night. The wicked recoil of each round kicked up a swirl of dust around the rocking chassis. Ejected round casings shot out from a chute in the rear of the turret and clattered on the ground. The M1128's were operating in batteries to concentrate their fire, scouring the slope of the far crest with canister. The thrashing hail forced the Russian infantry deep into their trenches, but did nothing to slow the rate of incoming mortar fire.

Caught exposed in soft cover, the dismounted Americans around the bridge died in their droves. Yet as troopers fell, so more men were flung forward into the crossfire of shrapnel and explosions. As the casualties rose, the Strykers on the road edged forward, keen to deflect some of the enemy's concentrated fire and give the troopers in the open small respite. One Stryker rushed onto the bridge behind a curtain of 50cal machine gun fire. A Russian RPG missile flashed across the night sky, missing the American vehicle and disappearing into a distant stand of trees. The Stryker's machine gun hammered the roadside on the far side of the bridge, rooting out enemy infantry that were firing from waist-deep trenches. Two Russians bounced up from the ditch and both men fired RPG's. The Stryker's hull was encased in a steel skirt of slat armor mounted to the sides of the vehicle, colloquially known as a 'bird cage'. The Stryker took two direct hits.

The slat armor was designed to detonate the piezo-electric fuse in the RPG's nose and misfocus the shaped charge jet. The Stryker shrugged off both rocket attacks and emerged from a dense wall of smoke scared and smoldering – but intact. The remote controlled 50cal machine gun in the turret turned and the two Russian soldiers disappeared in a roar of hammering revenge.

The Stryker remained on the bridge for several more seconds, allowing infantry to advance in its wake. Then the vehicle retreated behind a thick wall of smoke just as the distant sky erupted in a blooming flash of muzzle flame and a deafening *'crack!'*.

The round, fired by an unseen enemy from the saddle of the crest, missed the Stryker by a scant ten yards and struck one of the steel girders supporting the bridge. The night rung with a sound like a huge tolling bell. Then part of the bridge's twisted steel frame sagged into the river in a groaning agony of metal. The colossal noise seemed to stun the battlefield. The entire bridge became enveloped in thick boiling smoke. When the haze cleared the bridge still stood, and the Stryker had returned to the safety of the riverbank. More troopers swarmed forward, spilling from the back of their vehicles. Then the Russian mortar barrage resumed and in a matter of five cruel seconds the advancing troops were swatted down; shredded by a curtain of shrapnel explosions.

From the TOC, Colonel Sutcliffe watched the carnage on monitors with sinking despair. The feint assault was fast becoming a bloody slaughter. He turned to his aides, his eyes pricked with tears and his tone tortured.

"Where the fuck are the Polish? Why haven't they attacked the enemy's flank yet?"

*

"White One, White Two," Hal Calhoun's Texan drawl twanged over the Platoon net. "We have located and rendezvoused with the Polish Wolverines."

Edge snatched up the radio. "Where are you, Two?"

Calhoun rattled off a grid reference. Edge grabbed for a map and frowned. "You're still six clicks away, Two?"

"Confirm, One."

"What the hell are the Polish doing?"

"They've stopped, One."

"Stopped?"

"Confirm."

Edge felt his grip on the radio microphone tighten until his knuckles turned white.

"What the fuck did they stop for, Two?"

The static was filled with an incredulous pause. Finally Calhoun's voice came through the hiss and crackle. "One, the Polish Major halted the column because he was tired with a headache. He's been asleep for the past thirty minutes with orders that he cannot be disturbed."

Edge blinked. For a moment he was too stunned to speak. Then an unholy rage consumed him. He swore vehemently and bitterly, roaring an apoplectic litany of abuse that would have made a Paris whore blush. When he keyed the mike again his voice was low and icy with rage. "Two, fuck the Polish! Escort the three MGS's to the crossing, and if anyone tries to stop you, remind them the M1128's are not under Polish command. When you get here, we'll launch the attack ourselves if we have to."

"Confirm, One. We're on our way. Two out."

Calhoun's Stryker arrived at the river crossing eight minutes later. Behind him trailed the three MGS's, keeping open intervals to avoid the dust flung up by the preceding vehicle. Edge stood on the far riverbank with his hands propped on his hips.

"Bring them over!" he shouted across the water.

The vehicles went nose-first down the muddy bank. One by one they made the crossing, emerging on the far side streaming great torrents of water from their hulls. Edge directed Calhoun and the M1128's into the woods where Waddingham waited, but before they could move off a new roar of noise filled the night.

The ten remaining Polish Wolverines appeared out of the darkness. The lead vehicle had its driving lights blazing. Propped in the turret's command hatch, Major Nowakowski struck a warrior's heroic pose, his jaw thrust forward, his chin lifted with arrogant contempt. The vehicle braked to a halt by the river's muddy bank.

For two minutes nothing happened. Then, in a howl of revving engine noise and a billow of diesel exhaust, the KTO Rosomak lunged into the river, throwing up a wave of spray as it wallowed through the water. The vehicle slewed onto the far bank, its wheels spinning wildly, and came to a lurching stop.

From his lofty command perch, Major Nowakowski looked down on Edge and regarded him with haughty contempt.

"I am ready to lead our surprise attack to glorious victory," he announced loudly – but beneath the façade of bravado his face was a lather of nervous sweat, like that of a man sick with fear. He turned back to the river, his belly hanging against the rim of the hatch, and spoke into his headset. A moment later the second vehicle in the column slid down the slope of the riverbank like a skittish horse approaching a fence.

One by one the Wolverines made the crossing while Edge paced impatiently. In the background the sounds of the battle for the bridge intensified, emphasizing the critical importance of every second being wasted. Edge fumed at each small delay, seething with impatience. By the time the Polish vehicles were concealed within the woods he was so wild with frustration he could barely speak.

Nowakowski climbed ponderously down from his command vehicle and hitched up his pants with both elbows. He strutted importantly to Edge and regarded him with a condescending glare.

"My men are hungry. We will eat before we attack."

Edge flinched. A wave of murderous loathing overtook him. He had to resist the urge to cut the bastard's throat. "Can I speak to you in private, Major?" he snarled through gritted teeth.

He stalked into the woods until he was well out of earshot of the rest of the men. Major Nowakowski strutted behind him. Edge wheeled on the man and his pent-up fury exploded in a torrent of temper.

"Can you hear that, you bastard?" Edge flung his arm to the sky. "That's the sound of good men fighting and dying. They're being slaughtered at the bridge. Slaughtered – and it's been going on for thirty minutes! We should have been attacking by now. We should be crashing into the enemy's exposed flank. But we're not. And do you know why, you fucking arrogant ass? It's because of you! My friends are bleeding to death to buy us a chance to destroy the Russians. So shut your damned mouth about being hungry and get your men mounted up. We've got a fight to win and killing to be done."

Nowakowski's face turned ugly and swollen with insult. "You do not speak to me that way!" he blustered a protest. "I am a Major in the Polish Army, and I –"

"You're nothing but a primped up piece of shit!" Edge cut him off. "You've never seen combat in your life. You're an armchair general," he snarled in contempt. "You think I care about your rank? I don't. I care about the men on that bridge. Now, for the last time," he took a menacing step closer and there was cruel hatred in his eyes, "get your men in their vehicles and follow my scouts."

Shaken, trembling with outrage, the Polish Major stalked back through the woods.

Edge waited until he heard Nowakowski shout a flurry of orders to his men, then turned his head slowly. "Well? Did you hear that?"

Vince Waddingham emerged from the deep shadow of a nearby tree. He brushed leaves from his shoulders and smiled ruefully. "You really need to work on your people skills."

*

The 2nd Platoon Strykers were the first to move out, followed by the three MGS's and then the ten Polish Wolverines. Major Nowakowski stood mute and sullen in the hatch of his command vehicle, his face creased into a thunderous scowl.

Edge led the way northwest, crashing through the forest, throwing caution to the wind, and with every passing moment the horror of the bloody fight for the bridge grew louder and more intense.

Once inland of the river, the woods thinned and the canopy of trees overhead became patchy. The sky was filled with flashes of red fiery light and a thick pall of smoke. The sounds of fighting seemed to come in waves, like the crash of surf on a beach. Moments of chaotic intensity were followed by brief lulls – then another salvo would herald a renewed outburst of gunfire and the cycle repeated itself.

Standing in the command hatch of his Stryker, Edge counted down the minutes impatiently, urging the unwieldly column to greater speed – so that when the Stryker abruptly burst onto a pathway of clear ground he was taken by surprise.

"Driver, stop!"

They had reached the fire trail that he and Waddingham had traversed the night before. He leaped down from the Stryker and waved his arms, marshalling each vehicle as it appeared at the assembly point.

When Major Nowakowski's Wolverine emerged from the woods, Edge pointed to the west and spoke abruptly. "This is where we separate. Follow the fire trail. It will bring you out between the bridge and the saddle of the ridge. I will lead my column over the rise and behind the enemy's lines." He didn't wait for Nowakowski's acknowledgement. Instead he glanced at his watch. "I will be in position in ten minutes. That's when we launch our coordinated attack."

The Major lifted his chin in contemptible disregard and spoke into his headset. The Wolverine moved off at a cautious walking pace, followed by the rest of the Polish vehicles. Kalina appeared out of the darkened shadows.

"Can I fight with your men?" she asked Edge.

"Why?"

"I do not support the things my father has done…" she said no more.

Traversing the spine of the crest in the Strykers proved impossible. Edge was forced to lead his column on a circuitous route, skirting the foothills. He urged his driver to reckless speeds until they burst through a wall of ferns and onto the farm track. Suddenly the going was smooth and the path ahead clear. They raced towards the red-glowing sky, barely slowing as they passed the burned out shell of the Russian command vehicle Edge had destroyed with grenades. Another illumination round arced into the sky and burned bright as a star.

The dreadful crescendo of combat became deafening. Mortar rounds mingled with the throaty roar of heavy artillery to create a clamor of chaos. Edge checked his watch. There would be no time to form up or to organize a planned assault. It was to be a Cavalry charge in the traditional sense – a race into danger. In ninety seconds the Polish Wolverines would explode from the fringe of trees and fall upon the unsuspecting Russians. Edge had to be at the road to join the attack and to blockade any enemy attempt to retreat.

As the Strykers raced to meet their fate, it seemed to Edge, as it had in the past, that time slowed to a trickle. His mind picked out small details and registered them in startling clarity. He saw the crimson sky, glowing and pulsing from the flare of each new salvo, and he heard the fluting whine of a mortar shell as it reached the zenith of its trajectory and then plummeted back towards earth. He saw the end of the farm track blocked by an old wooden gate and bordered on both sides by a high wall of trees. Beyond the fence he saw the ghostly shadows of movement; it might have been Russian infantry or perhaps a small vehicle. Then he heard the wicked *'crack!'* of a high-caliber muzzle, and a moment later a huge explosion.

"Faster!" he urged his driver as fear and the exhilaration of imminent danger descended upon him. *"Charge!"*

*

Everything happened during the few wild seconds the Strykers dashed along the farm track.

Edge's gunner and vehicle commander climbed up through his hatch to stand at the 50cal machine gun, while in the buttoned-up troop compartment Waddingham, Kalina, and his three scout team members made final hasty checks of their weapons.

Waddingham had his eyes glued to the navigation computer. Blue dots marked the positions of all four vehicles in the Platoon, projected onto a satellite map of the local terrain.

Waddingham passed around a clutch of additional grenades to his team as the image on the monitor blinked and then refreshed.

"Stay alert," Waddingham told his team. On the screen he could see the Stryker's position drawing inexorably closer to the road. "Once we clear the farm track, the ramp is gonna come down. We exit hard and fast. Everything is an enemy target. Our objective is to find and neutralize the Russian mortars."

The three MGS's had been designated Green Platoon. Edge issued last minute instructions over the net to each of the vehicles and then switched frequencies to contact command. "Checkmate Six Romeo, this is Outlaw White One. We are in position and launching our flank attack in ten seconds. Over."

"This is Checkmate Six Romeo. Roger." The operator at the TOC replied. The radio stayed hot for a few seconds longer and then abruptly cut off. Edge let go of the transmission switch and ducked his head down into the hull of the Stryker. He made eye contact with Vince Waddingham. "We'll cover you with the 50cal as far as the foothills of the ridge. From there you're on your own."

Waddingham acknowledged with a thumbs-up.

Edge climbed back up through the hatch just as the Stryker reached the wooden gate. The brittle timber exploded in a spray of splinters. The Stryker jounced over a patch of loose gravel driveway and then up onto the camber of the road with a savage jolt that cracked Edge's teeth together. The vehicle slewed across the blacktop and, even before it had come to a complete stop, the rear ramp began descending.

"Go! Go! Go!"

The four scouts and Kalina burst from the belly of the Stryker and scrambled across the road into long grass. Over their heads the 50cal thundered to life. The Stryker was stationery, facing back towards the saddle of the ridge and, beyond it, the river.

They were behind the enemy's lines.

Edge had expected the world to be a thunder of explosions and chattering machine gun fire as the startled Russians reacted to the crashing arrival of the Polish on their flank, yet everything seemed drowned out by the fury of the 50cal. Its flickering tongue of flame lit the night as the gunner sprayed a hedgerow.

The other vehicles in the attack split north and south. The MGS's surged up the rise towards the saddle of the ridge. The three remaining Platoon scout vehicles raced north to blockade any attempted Russian retreat. It happened so fast that Edge barely had time to draw a breath.

Then, at last, the Russians fought back.

From a trench by the side of the road a Russian soldier leaped to his feet with an RPG on his shoulder. He took aim at the lead MGS and fired broadside at the target from less than fifty yards. The vehicle was protected by a 'bird cage' steel skirt around its hull which diffused the impact of the rocket. The slatted armor saved the M1128 from destruction but not damage. It disappeared in a huge rolling cloud of smoke and flames. When the haze cleared, the left side of the Stryker was down on the ground, three of its wheels blown from their axles. The vehicle ground to a juddering halt and seemed to 'brew up'. Smoke billowed from the ruined carcass and then flickering tongues of orange flame licked along the underside of the hull. The vehicle's steel hatches swung open and crewmen scrambled to safety. Russian automatic fire cut the troopers down and left them dead on the blacktop.

Edge watched on in helpless horror. He seized the gunner's arm in the turret beside him and directed fire at the Russian trenches. The 50cal swung onto its new target and the grassy verge dissolved into clods of flung earth and smoke.

Fresh enemy fire erupted from the ridgeline and then a grenade exploded nearby. Russian soldiers darted across the road, hidden behind skeins of smoke and firing from the hip as they moved. Automatic gunfire flashed and thundered. Enemy machine gun bullets clanged like a blacksmith's hammer off the hull of Edge's Striker. A Russian soldier went down in the middle of the blacktop, clutching at his stomach. His helmet fell from his head and rolled into the grass.

"Get off the road!" Edge shouted to his driver. The vehicle reversed, turned, then crashed through the hedgerow. Vince Waddingham and the other scouts were lying prone behind cover, pinned down by a Russian machine gun, while further along the slope of the ridge, through a fringe of trees, Edge glimpsed the enemy's mortars and the silhouette of a transport truck. The mortars appeared to be operating from a tree-encircled clearing at the foot of the hill, raining hell down on the men attacking the bridge and unaware that Edge was hunting them.

"Hit that machine gun with everything you've got!" Edge ordered his gunner. The 50cal swung on its mount and sprayed a shuddering hail of gunfire. Edge leaped down from the Stryker with his M4 in his hand. Waddingham looked woefully in his direction.

"What are we doing?"

"We're going forward. We have to get to the mortars." Edge ran at a crouch, boots scrabbling for purchase in the long muddy grass. Waddingham and Kalina sprang to their feet and the other scouts followed. The Russian machine gun post was deeply entrenched. It fired back at the Stryker's gunner, forcing the man to duck behind cover.

"Christ!" Edge realized the sudden danger but knew there was no alternative other than to keep running. They were hopelessly exposed and still the Russian machine gun fired. One of Waddingham's scouts was struck in the shoulder. The impact of the round spun him sideways and then a second bullet knocked him dead to the ground. Waddingham saw the man fall but could do nothing. He gritted his teeth and forced himself on up the slope until his lungs were bursting and his breath sawed in his throat.

At the moment Edge was certain the machine gunner would traverse his aim and target him, the 50cal mounted atop the Stryker opened fire again. Edge threw himself face-down into the dirt as the bullets roared over his head. He heard a short, sharp scream of pain and when he lifted his eyes the Russian machine gun post had dissolved into a furrow of churned earth.

"Fire in the hole!" Waddingham shouted and hurled a grenade. The trench erupted outwards in an avalanche of loose earth and dust. Before the smoke had settled Edge was on his feet. He dashed up the slope and stood poised on the rim of the crater. Both the Russians were dead.

He dropped into a crouch and Waddingham joined him, his chest heaving like a bellows. Both men were dripping with sweat. "The job's not done," Edge insisted savagely. "We have to reach those mortar crews and kill the bastards!"

*

Major Nowakowski stood in the shadows of the forest and stared cautiously through the veil of foliage at the horror unfolding across the battlefield. Under the flare of glowing illumination rounds and fiery explosions the fight for the bridge resembled a luridly-lit glimpse of Hell.

The Russian mortars were in a fury, turning the ground around the crossing into a churned muddy graveyard. The air seemed to quiver and quake with automatic gunfire.

He stayed hidden and watched aghast as three Russian soldiers crept through long grass to the edge of the road and then bounced to their feet to fire on stranded American soldiers. Several Cavalry troopers were hit in the fusillade. One man who had been kneeling behind a twist of metal wreckage cried out in agony and threw his arms in the air. He had been shot in the head. He tumbled from the bridge and splashed dead into the water below.

The Major's face blanched white with fear. His stomach felt knotted and his breath came in shallow whimpers. A wayward mortar shell landed in the river, throwing up a great fountain of water. Then the American M1128's launched a salvo of counter fire. A sudden hellish glow lit the skyline and a moment later the air overhead seemed to crack apart with thunder. A muscle in the Major's cheek twinged and his legs turned to jelly. The American rounds landed on the crest, about halfway up the slope. The ridge had been horribly mauled by shellfire so that no vegetation remained and all that stood were the blackened stumps of shattered trees surrounded by deep muddy shell craters. The ground trembled as each round exploded and the night was lit bright by the flare of their fireballs. The air smelled of cordite and blood and death and smoke. The thunder of the explosions rolled away on the breeze, leaving Major Nowakowski with dulled senses and singing eardrums.

The agonized cry of a Russian dying before his eyes roused the Major back to alertness. The soldier was lying on the road, writhing in agony. He had been shot in the leg and was bleeding profusely. He called out to a comrade, his voice pleading, but no one came to his aid. The Major watched until the man stopped moving and lay dead on the blacktop.

A sudden hand on his shoulder made him cry out in whimpering terror. He turned wide-eyed, his mouth hanging slack with fright.

"Forgive me, Major," the Polish Captain apologized. "It is time. Sergeant Edge's Stryker column has already begun to engage the enemy. We must launch our attack to support them."

Nowakowski shrugged the man's hand from his shoulder. In an instant a mask of bravado replaced his look of fear. He glowered at the Captain and snorted.

"Do not presume to tell me of military strategy," he growled. "How do you know the Strykers are attacking?"

"We have been monitoring the American radios, Major," The Captain explained. "They attacked at the agreed time…" he glanced at his watch, "…and have been fighting without us for several minutes."

"I have changed my mind," the Major said.

"Sir?" the Captain looked appalled.

"We will not launch an attack. To do so would be folly. A child can see that the Russians are too deeply entrenched and too well prepared to be shifted from their position. The American Colonel is a poor tactician and has been punished for his naivety. I will not be a part of his folly, nor will I risk Polish military vehicles."

"But we vowed to support the Americans…" the Captain persisted.

"Let them die," Nowakowski's tone was scornful. "It is exactly what Sergeant Edge and his men deserve."

He looked again out through the veil of trees. "At any moment the Russians are going to push the Americans back off the bridge with RPG and mortar fire. Then they will turn on Edge and crush him," he clenched his fist to emphasize his claim. "The Americans will be ignominiously defeated. The men on the far side of the bridge will retreat. Edge and his band of fools will be killed or forced to surrender. If we engage the enemy, we will do nothing but expose ourselves to the American failure. No!" he shook his head. "A thousand times no! We will withdraw. We will fall back across the river and select a strong defensive position from where we can stop the Russians from advancing any further."

"But Major, the Russians are not interested in advancing. They are interested only in preventing an allied flank attack against their Warsaw-bound spearhead."

Nowakowski regarded the man with contemptuous scorn. "You are an idiot!"

The Captain flinched and dissolved into red-faced silence.

"The Russians will attack across the bridge once the American thrust has been broken on their guns," Nowakowski prophesized. "Have you learned nothing of warfare? Do they not teach grand strategy in our military academies? The Russians will come pouring across the Sypitki and the Americans will be too demoralized and dispirited to resist them. The only way to defend our homeland is to keep our Army intact."

He could still salvage something from the American debacle, the Polish Major decided, but he had to act quickly.

He must withdraw to the far bank of the river before the Russians discovered his column and turned their fury on him.

"Return to the vehicles," Nowakowski ordered the Captain. "And get the troops mounted up. We will retire immediately."

Chapter 9:

Edge drew the rest of the group around him and looked at them. They were all breathing hard, their faces coated with dust and spattered mud, cut through with runnels of sweat. Their eyes were bloodshot and bleary.

"We have to take out the mortars," Edge explained, pointing further along the slope. From where they were crouched the enemy was out of sight behind a palisade of low trees, but the repetitive cough of their incessant firing carried clearly. "Until we silence those bastards, the men around the bridge are going to keep dying. But there's only four of us, and there's at least eighteen of them." Edge had seen at least half a dozen Russian field mortars, and knew each weapon would be serviced by at least three men. Then there were the support troops to consider. He had seen the bulky outline of at least one troop truck parked on the fringe of the clearing, but there could be more. "So this might be a suicide mission…" he said.

"You forgot about me," Kalina said stiffly. "I can fight. I've proven myself."

Edge shook his head. "I'm not doubting your bravery or your skill. But we get paid to do this work. You're part-time militia. You need to head back to the road and find our Strykers barricading the Russian retreat. You'll be safest there."

Kalina's expression darkened and her eyes turned smoldering. She glowered but said nothing.

Edge got to his feet and turned away. Waddingham and his two remaining scouts moved off with him into the flickering darkness. They moved with stealthy caution, climbing higher up the slope of the ridge as they closed on the fringe of trees that sheltered the mortar teams. The sound of the Russian crews working their weapons became louder. Edge could hear their barked commands, the metronomic repetition of orders, and mechanical actions that kept the deadly weapons constantly firing. Tendrils of grey smoke twisted between the trees and through it glowed the flickering bright flash of each round blasting into the night sky.

As they crept closer, Edge found himself praying that the Russians would not detect them, praying that the sounds of fighting and the loose cloak of darkness would conceal their movement.

Fifty yards from the barricade of trees, Edge called a halt and sank down onto his haunches. The scouts formed a knot around him and leaned close. A flicker of dark movement caught his eye. Edge glanced over his shoulder and cursed.

"I told you not to follow us. I told you to join the Strykers."

"I am not under your orders," Kalina stepped into a glimmer of light. Her jaw was set in a stubborn line of defiance and her eyes were hard with resolve. "So you either include me in your plan, or I attack the mortars alone."

Edge muttered an oath under his breath and sighed in resignation. Kalina pushed her way in close to the others.

The Russians still fired, still serviced their weapons with slavish dedication, while from the road behind them the sounds of battle reached a crescendo. Edge could hear the Russian mortar crews clearly, and even distinguish the differences between individual voices. A fresh salvo of mortar rounds flashed into the night sky, followed by a billow of swirling grey smoke. A burst of Russian radio chatter cut through the night.

"Sergeant, you me and Kalina will go forward into the trees and make the attack," Edge spoke to Waddingham. "You guys," he singled out the remaining two scouts, "will destroy the trucks. There's at least one parked in the woods to the north, but there might be more."

They separated. Edge led Waddingham and Kalina to the stand of trees, creeping cautiously closer. They crawled through the undergrowth until the mortar park was in sight.

The clearing was an oval area, fifty yards across, bordered on every side by woods and bushes. Two troop trucks were parked with their tarpaulin-covered cargo bays facing the clearing from which a steady procession of soldiers frantically unloaded ammunition. The weapons were set in a line, separated by a waist-high redoubt of sandbags, each mortar braced on a steel bipod frame, their tubes elevated into the smoke-filled sky.

Edge crawled forward until he was laying concealed on the fringe of the clearing. Waddingham and Kalina lay in the scrubby undergrowth beside him. Edge did a head-count.

"Twenty three that I can see, including the officer," he pointed to a man who stood separate from the mortars clutching a hand-held radio. He was a tall bull of a man with a barrel chest and a stern fleshy face.

"They're not good odds," Vince Waddingham understated gloomily.

"We're going to have to take out as many as we can in the first few seconds and then get in close to finish them – ".

A Russian soldier standing by one of the lorries reached into the tray of the truck for another mortar round and then stopped suddenly. His eyes flashed wide with shock and he shouted a warning.

"Amerikantsy!"

"Shit!" Edge cursed. The two scouts working their way closer to the trucks had been spotted. For a moment nothing happened. Then the tall Russian officer bellowed a string of urgent orders and the Russians scrambled to retrieve weapons.

A sudden violent explosion shook the night. One of the trucks erupted in a ball of flame and smoke, blown apart by two grenades. Then a rattle of automatic fire cut down two Russians near the north side of the clearing.

"Fire!" Edge shouted.

Beside the closest mortar Edge could see the startled three-man crew freeze, and then dive for their weapons. One of the soldiers ducked behind the barrier of sandbags and came up firing wildly. The bullets ripped through the trees well to Edge's right and disappeared into the night. A pistol shot cracked. Edge sprayed the mortar position with automatic fire from his M4. Waddingham and Kalina opened fire a split-second later and the clearing turned into a charnel house.

Edge knew their attack had to be determined and ferocious. He couldn't let the battle turn into a firefight; he couldn't allow the Russians time to find cover and organize resistance. Impulsively he leaped to his feet; Waddingham was at his shoulder, firing from the hip, and the two men screamed a wild challenge as they broke from cover and charged. The night lit up with gouts of chattering flame, Edge saw two Russians fold forward clutching at gaping stomach wounds, and then the hot breath of a bullet flashed past his cheek, missing by mere inches. Edge turned and saw a Russian mortarman behind a sandbag wall aiming an AK-74 at him. He fired and the man disappeared in a spray of blood. Another tall Russian lunged at him from out of the dark, knocking him to the ground, and he rolled away just as the glint of a knife whizzed past his ear. He kicked out at the man who went staggering backwards, his arms cartwheeling in the air for a handhold that wasn't there. Edge scrambled for his M4 and fired from his knees, hitting the man in the chest. Waddingham fired at the same instant. The Russian jerked like a puppet on a string from the fusillade of hits and was dead before he struck the ground. The Russian officer commanding the post threw down his radio and bellowed at Edge, reaching for the pistol holstered on his hip. Waddingham leaped into the space between them and fired. The Russian officer stumbled backwards under the impact of several bullets and Waddingham followed through with a savage kick that caught the big man under the jaw and broke every tooth in his mouth.

"Jesus!" Edge gasped. He heaved himself to his feet and then ducked again instinctively as Russians in the far mortar pit fired indiscriminately into the melee of scrambling, snarling mayhem. The bullets thudded into sandbags with a meaty 'thwack'. Edge crawled six paces to his left and then bounced to his feet, the M4 shuddering in his hands as he sprayed the Russians with a swathe of fire until the magazine in his weapon clicked empty. A violent explosion shook the ground and a fireball erupted around the second truck. Edge heard Kalina scream and turned in alarm as he reloaded. But it was not a scream of pain. It was a wild rage of noise in the back of her throat as she shot a Russian from point bank range then reversed the weapon in a berserk fury and clubbed him across the face with the stock. Blood sprayed from the man's mouth and the crack of his jaw breaking sounded just as loudly as the automatic fire that rattled across the night. Several of the Russians threw down their weapons, appalled and terrified, and fled panicked into the trees. One of Edge's scouts stepped out of the woods to fire on a man hiding behind a sandbag. He missed, and the Russian returned fire, hitting the scout in the pelvis. The Cavalryman sagged to his knees and fired again, then fell dead to the dirt. Waddingham fired then wrenched himself out of the way of a man who came at him with bunched brawling fists. He ducked a punch that would have separated his head from his shoulders and then drew his bayonet and buried it hilt-deep into the Russian's thigh. He went down howling in agony. Waddingham swung his M4 and shot him between the eyes. Kalina leaped a wall of sandbags and cannoned into a mortarman. They fell in an awkward tumble of arms and legs. The gun in the man's hands clattered into the dirt. Kalina turned on him like a trapped savage lioness, her eyes wild. She sank her teeth into the man's cheek and he rolled away screaming, a high-pitched sound in his throat like a steam kettle. Edge had a full magazine and he used it to scythe down three Russians in a mortar pit, a blood-curdling roar of savagery in his throat as each man fell dead. Then he was faced with a Russian wielding a weapon like a club. Edge tried to swing the M4 onto the man's center mass but he was too close, charging forward with a formless incoherent cry of fury in his throat. He swung his AK-74 like an axe and hit Edge flush on the shoulder. Pain exploded in pinwheels of bright light through the top of his skull. He staggered sideways and the man hunted him, kicking Edge in the ribs. Edge doubled over. A billow of dust clouded the air from his dragging boots and then Waddingham was there again with his M4, snarling. He shot the Russian in the face and the man's head snapped back, his skull collapsing in a custard-colored mist of blood and gore. The second scout was dead on the ground, lying in a pool of dark blood. A Russian tripped over the man's lifeless legs and scrambled backwards over the blood-slippery ground, pleading for mercy as Waddingham hunted him.

"Nyet! Miloserdiye!"

Waddingham shot the man in the chest, raised his M4 two inches and shot another man who had turned to flee into the woods. The Russian cried out and clutched at his arm but kept running. Kalina saw the exchange and dashed into the woods after the wounded man. He darted in and out of view, disappearing into a dark shadow of forest. Then suddenly there were no more Russians to fight, no more enemy to be killed. The abrupt silence was not complete, but very nearly so. Men moaned in agony, others writhed on the ground, or clawed at the earth, dragging their broken bodies through smears of their own blood, pleading for help. One Russian lay in a doubled-over heap in the dirt and retched quietly, his hands trying to staunch a bleeding gut wound.

"Jesus!" Edge gasped. He slumped against a blood-spattered sandbag, his chest heaving. His left side was numb, his arm hanging useless at his side. He was standing in a pool of blood, but it wasn't his. The clearing had been turned to a mud-churned slaughterhouse, blanketed in smoke from the two burning transport trucks. Edge drew a deep breath and looked, numb and bleary-eyed, at the horrific carnage.

"You alright?" Waddingham emerged from the haze, M4 in his hand. He was covered in dust. Kalina appeared from behind one of the burning trucks. She walked like she was in a daze, her eyes glassy.

Edge nodded, sucked in a deep breath and gasped again, "Jesus!"

The clearing was a gruesome abattoir of blood and gore. Everywhere Edge looked he saw fresh horror. He scraped the back of his hand across his mouth. His fingers were trembling.

Vince Waddingham stared at the dead bodies in silent appalled shock. The entire battle had lasted less than a single savage minute. "Now what?" he croaked.

"We need to climb to the top of the ridge," Edge rasped. "I have to see what's happening and find out why the Russians are still fighting. The battle should be over. The Russians should have surrendered by now. Something's gone horribly wrong and I need to know what it is."

*

"Stay low and keep alert," Edge warned as they began to climb the slope.

"You think there's still Russians alive up there after all the fire the M1128's poured onto that ridge?" Waddingham asked.

"There might be," Edge said, working the numbness from his arm by flexing his fingers. "Let's not find out the hard way."

At first the going was relatively easy. Although some of the American shrapnel and HEAT rounds had overshot onto the reverse slope of the ridge, most of the low-lying foothills remained sparsely forested. But as they continued to climb, the earth turned lumped and cratered, and the incline grew steeper.

They intersected a boot-worn track that followed a rocky spine, winding towards the summit over hard ground. On either side of the trail the earth had been churned into a quagmire. As they approached the summit, the upper slopes were denuded of foliage so the crest of the ridge resembled a desolate moonscape. The mutilated bodies of Russian soldiers lay half-buried in the mire, their trenches blown apart by direct hits, their corpses shredded by the flail of shrapnel canisters. The stump of a dismembered arm thrust up out of the ground, and nearby a young soldier lay dead. The blast of an explosion had shredded the uniform from his body. His remains were slashed with dozens of cruel wounds, his face a pulp of mangled flesh. There were others too. They were no longer recognizable as human. They lay in gruesome poses, their gas-filled, wound-riddled bodies already turning purple and bloating. A crow picked greedily at the remains, cawing noisomely at Edge as he passed.

Edge dropped to his knee when they reached the skyline and waited for the flash of an explosion to light up the battlefield. He was breathing hard.

The American M1128's were still pounding the ridge with HEAT. Three rounds landed further down the slope and a fourth crashed in the field between the foothills and the dark ribbon of road. For several seconds the battlefield below him was lit in lurid orange flashes of light. Edge stared, and for a long moment nothing made sense. Then the sick realization struck, and a red mist of rage consumed him.

"The fucking Polish haven't attacked!" he croaked. His voice was incredulous with disbelief. "The bastard! Oh, the cowardly fucking bastard. Nowakowski let us launch the attack on our own. He's still hiding in the fucking forest!"

Waddingham knelt beside Edge and peered into the fading darkness. The night below was streaked with tracer fire that arced across the night and lit by the muzzle flashes of machine guns.

"Are you sure?"

"Yes!" Edge hissed. Ten seconds later Waddingham and Kalina saw for themselves. As the next barrage of American HEAT rounds peppered the foothills, the gloom was lit in bright flashes of light that showed the road littered with dead bodies, debris and the smoldering ruins of Strykers. But the Polish Wolverines were nowhere to be seen.

"The bastard!" Vince Waddingham hissed.

Kalina gaped, stunned and disbelieving. In the fading glow of the explosions her face looked pale with shock.

"I'm going to murder the bastard!" Edge swore bitterly.

"Cover me as far as the road," Kalina rose to her feet. "I will find out where the Wolverines are."

"You can't," Edge pulled her down into a shell crater of erupted earth. "You won't make it alive. Vince and I will do it. We need those Wolverines and we need those Polish soldiers in the fight."

"I am going," Kalina shook his hand away. Her eyes were hard as stone. "I'm the only one my father might listen to."

*

With Edge and Waddingham providing overwatch from a shell crater on the crest of the ridge, Kalina went down the slope at a run. Using the darkness for cover she ghosted into the night, moving like a wraith. Edge and Waddingham lost sight of her as she reached the foothills of the slope. Two more massive explosions landed half-way up the ridge, forcing both men to duck instinctively. When they lifted their heads above the lip of the crater, Kalina was nowhere to be seen.

"Come on," Edge led the way. "We need to get to the saddle of this ridge and join the fight."

Edge and Waddingham rose cautiously and began to make their way along the spine of the crest towards the road. They went doubled-over, careful not to leave themselves silhouetted against the skyline. Edge used the flickering light to pick a winding path across the battle-churned ground.

Then suddenly the earth fell away into a deep dark hole. Edge teetered on the lip of the pit. A Russian soldier was laying on his back in the bottom of the trench. His young mud-smeared face was pale with fear. He saw Edge and threw up his weapon instinctively.

"Amerikanets!"

The young soldier fired into the night, hitting Edge flush in the chest. The impact of the bullet hurled him backwards. Edge fell to the ground, writhing and cursing in pain. Vince Waddingham saw Edge fall.

"Jesus!" He plucked a grenade from his webbing belt and dropped it into the trench, then flung himself on top of Edge's prone body to shield him from the blast. The earth shuddered like a living thing. Chunks of dirt showered them in heavy clods, choked them in thick veils of dust.

"Are you okay?" Waddingham pounded Edge's shoulder and slapped him across the face. "Are you hit? Are you hurt?"

With frantic fingers he searched Edge's body for wounds, for a warm wet rush of blood. He could find nothing.

Edge clutched at his chest, rolled onto his side and coughed. The pain burned through his body. He drew his knees up to his stomach and lay wheezing in the night.

"Were you hit?" Waddingham asked urgently.

Edge sat up slowly and winced. He tore at the Velcro straps that secured his body armor vest and felt inside his jacket. Beneath his exploring fingers he discovered a lump the size of a fist. The bullet had struck him in the torso mid-way between his chest and navel on the right-hand side. The armor had saved his life. He winced again and drew a shallow shuddering breath.

Waddingham sat down in the dirt and sighed his relief. "That's gonna leave a nasty bruise," he gloated.

Edge got unsteadily to his feet. Waddingham helped him refit his body armor. Edge's ears were ringing. His torso felt like a shirt full of bruises.

"Your turn to be a target," he croaked. "You can lead the way. We have to keep going towards the saddle of the ridge."

Waddingham nodded. "Follow me – and try not to get shot again."

*

The troops were clambering aboard the Wolverines. The vehicles had been turned around and were lined in a column on the fire trail, facing back the way they had come. Major Nowakowski stood with two aides by his command vehicle, impatient to withdraw before the Russians discovered them.

Kalina burst through the screen of trees at the fringe of the woods and stared aghast. She ran towards her father, a turmoil of emotions and conflict.

"What are you doing?"

Major Nowakowski seemed tense and anxious. He turned on Kalina. His eyes were hectic. He saw the accusation on her face and tried to mollify her.

"I am doing what is best for Poland," the Major said stiffly. "I am making the hard decision that will secure our nation's future."

"No!" Kalina protested. Nowakowski reached for her but she shook his hands away angrily. "No! You're making the coward's decision. Our allies are fighting and dying beyond those trees to secure our nation's future. You are thinking only of yourself."

The Major's eyes hardened. His voice cracked like a whip.

"You have no right to speak to me that way. I am your commanding officer and you are a member of the Polish *Wojska Obrony Terytorialnej.*"

"You are a coward!" the word came into her throat like an involuntary exclamation of pain.

Major Nowakowski slapped Kalina across the face. The air between them crackled with fraught tension. Then something seemed to die in Kalina's eyes. She backed away, her expression pure loathing. She spun on her heel and went running back along the line of Wolverines. Suddenly she was shouting, her voice lifted so every soldier could hear.

"Brave Polish warriors! Our American allies are beyond that wall of trees dying for us. They're laying down their lives to keep Poland free from Russian occupation. Will you fight with them? Or will you slink away into the night like our cowardly commander? Who amongst you is man enough to take the war to the Russians alongside me?"

"Arrest her!" Major Nowakowski bellowed in a fit of rage. He shoved one of his aides towards his daughter. "Arrest her now!"

As Kalina ran along the line of armored vehicles she bashed her fist against each steel hull, rousing the soldiers inside. They came out into the night, grim-faced with weapons in their hands.

"Follow me!" Kalina shouted. "The battle is almost won. With one brave attack we can crush the Russians and drive them back."

"No!" Major Nowakowski barked. "You soldiers have your orders. Get into the vehicles. We depart in three minutes."

"In three minutes this battle can be won!" Kalina defied her father. "In three minutes you can all be heroes. The choice is yours. Will you live as cowards for the rest of your lives, or will you fight bravely beside the Americans who are dying for you?"

The militia followed her, buoyed by a groundswell of patriotic fervor. A ragged cheer rose in their throats and became a roar. The Polish *Wojska Obrony Terytorialnej* burst from the tree line with their guns blazing.

They were going to war.

At last.

*

"We're going down there," Edge told Waddingham, pointing to a knoll of cratered ground that overhung the saddle of the ridge. From the craggy outcrop he would have an unobstructed view of the road all the way back to the bridge and all the way north to where his Strykers were positioned to barricade a Russian retreat.

"It's going to get noisy," Waddingham said. They were moving closer to the heart of the battle. "And dangerous."

Edge went cautiously in the dark, using the flicker of fresh explosions to light the rugged path, past trenches that had been destroyed in the American bombardment, past the bodies of dead enemy soldiers who had defended the ridge. The Russians were fighting fiercely, concentrating around the rise in the road. The soldiers who had endured the murderous direct fire barrage from the M1128's had evidently gravitated towards the defensive strongpoint and were fighting with desperate determination. They were dug in on both sides of the pass and in ditches along the verge of the woods.

Then Edge heard a ragged cheer above the clamor of the firefight, and a mass of Polish militia rushed from the dense forest out into the night.

The surprised Russians opened fire.

The enemy were deeply entrenched in narrow ditches, safe behind earthen redoubts or shooting from behind sandbag walls. A roar of automatic gunfire ripped the night apart, and grenades flew through the air. The crash of explosions became endless. Somehow the Polish infantry withstood the fusillade and closed on the Russian trenches. Hand-to-hand fighting broke out. Polish militia leaped into the ditches and fought with knives and bare hands, overwhelming their enemy. Others hurled grenades into the deep pits. Some of the Russians cowered in their trenches, firing blindly over their heads. Others broke from their cover and retreated. The bravest stood their ground and fired defiantly until their weapons ran out of ammunition. Then the Polish Wolverines burst from the forest. Nine of the armored personnel carriers crashed into the Russian flank, their 30mm chain guns blazing.

Edge stood on the knoll of high ground overlooking the road and was overcome with a wave of relief.

The road was open to the Polish and the first of the Wolverines dashed for the crest, but a Russian-fired RPG blew the vehicle apart. The rocket struck the side of the Wolverine as it raced past a trench. The personnel carrier exploded behind a firestorm of flames and smoke. The vehicle careened off the road and into an empty ditch, trailing smoke and fire. A second Wolverine surged forward and it seemed that the Polish would overwhelm the last of the Russian defenders. The vehicle's engine howled, belching black clouds of diesel exhaust as it gained speed.

The rise of the road was consumed in a new fireball of flashing light and a booming *'crack!'* of thunder.

Edge saw it all.

There were two Russian T-90 tanks parked on either side of the pass at the point where the road crested the saddle of the ridge. The tanks were hull-down behind three-sided sandbag redoubts, camouflaged to conceal their location. The first T-90 fired on the advancing Wolverine from a range of less than two hundred yards and immolated it. The earth shook. The tongue of flame from the Russian tank's muzzle leaped thirty feet from the barrel, lighting up the night. The Wolverine was so close that the sound of the tank firing and the appalling crash of the vehicle exploding seemed to blend into a single maelstrom of sound.

"Christ Almighty!" Vince Waddingham gasped.

A moment of stunned silence seemed to envelope the battlefield. Then the second T-90 revealed its position, opening fire on a Wolverine that had slewed off the road to seek cover. The garish flash of the shot lit up the night and the Wolverine took a direct hit that ripped it apart. The Polish infantry began to falter, assailed by infantry and armor. Some of them edged back towards the trees. Others flung themselves down into abandoned enemy trenches.

The Russian infantry recognized the sudden shift of momentum. They dashed forward, firing from the hip, and drove the Polish back. It looked like a scene from hell; flashes of muzzle flame stabbing into the dark, blooms of exploding light among the trees, and the moans of men dying, shrieking in agony. The militia began to retreat, going deep into the woods to escape the fury of the determined counter attack. Machine gun fire followed them, slashing through leaves and thudding into tree trunks.

"They've broken," Edge groaned as he watched the Polish flee, shattered and in disorder. The militia's charge had failed, leaving the battlefield layered in dense veils of smoke. It twisted in tendrils through the trees and it cloaked the bodies that lay dead and dying. The stench of cordite hung in the air.

Waddingham stared into the chaos, bereft and despairing – and saw something move in the distance. It came from the far side of the rise, moving through the smoke towards the ridge. He seized Edge's arm and pointed.

Edge held his breath.

The American M1128 MGS burst through the haze a hundred yards shy of the crest and took aim on the rear of a T-90. The MGS carried the same 105mm cannon that had been fitted to the original version of the Abrams main battle tank. In a prolonged firefight with a T-90, the thin-skinned MGS was woefully under gunned – but against the Russian tank's vulnerable rear armor from close range, the 105mm cannon could wreak havoc.

The MGS lurched to a sudden halt in the middle of the road and opened fire. The recoil of the massive blast rocked the Stryker on its suspension so it swayed like a boat on a storm-tossed sea. The sabot round crashed into the rear of the T-90 and consumed the tank in a thick choking billow of smoke and dust. But when the haze began to clear, the Russian tank was undamaged, and its turret began turning to hunt the MGS. The Stryker fired a second round, and this time the sabot dart penetrated the Russian tank's thin rear armor. The T-90 erupted in fire, thrown forward on its steel tracks by the impact so it seemed to lurch behind a wall of fierce flame. Two of the vehicle's crew bailed out of the burning vehicle through the turret hatch but were gunned down by Polish infantry.

The second T-90 reversed from behind its redoubt. The tank's heavy steel tracks shredded the blacktop as the vast steel beast trundled onto the road. It fired on the MGS and obliterated the American Stryker, the wicked whip-crack of its main gun splitting the dark night apart.

Edge sensed the assault hung precariously in the balance. "The other MGS needs to get into the fight before that T-90 can turn the tide of battle."

Vince Waddingham had a better idea.

Chapter 10:

"Follow me!" Waddingham turned and went down the slope of the knoll like a mountain goat. "We've got to get to one of the Wolverines."

Edge ran in Waddingham's wake. His gear flapped and banged about his waist as he leaped a shell crater. He jinked left to avoid the corpse of a dead Russian soldier who had been decapitated during the American bombardment. Sweat streamed into his eyes, and the weight of his body armor felt like an anchor. His injured chest hurt fiercely with every step but he gritted his teeth and pushed himself on.

"That one!" Waddingham pointed to the trees on the far side of the road where a Wolverine stood, half-concealed in the gloom. The vehicle had crashed nose-first into a Russian trench and been abandoned by its crew. It was canted drunkenly to one side, the rear doors of its empty troop compartment swinging open.

"Come on!" Waddingham reached the verge of the road and ran, doubled over into a fusillade of crossfire. Bullets gouged at the blacktop around his feet, ricocheted off twisted steel wreckage and flew past his ears. Arcs of white tracer reached out for him, hunting his fleeting shape as he dashed into danger. Edge followed. The road was a charnel of bloodied bodies. Some lay on the blacktop as dark unmoving lumps, others screamed their pain.

"Run!" Waddingham shouted. Once across the road he dropped to his knee and returned fire on the Russians. Edge ran as if the devil was on his heels. He angled his sprint across the open road, weaving between the carnage. A Polish militia officer standing waist-high in an abandoned trench mistook Edge for a Russian and fired at him in blind panic. Edge felt the bullet's hot passage pass so close to his cheek that he staggered.

"I'm American, you stupid bastard!" Edge bellowed the reproof.

"Russians on the right!" Waddingham shouted the warning and Edge threw himself to the ground as Waddingham opened fire. Two Russians had come down from the crest of the road, hunting the Polish militia as they retreated. Waddingham shot them both. Edge saw the first Russian twist as three bullets struck him in the groin. It seemed, for an instant, that his legs buckled. Then he toppled forward into the dirt, screaming in pain. The second Russian tried to duck for cover as Waddingham swung his weapon onto him. The soldier threw himself to the right, towards a patch of dark shadow, but a hail of bullets caught him in mid-flight. He dropped to the dirt like a shot bird and didn't move again.

"Get up! Run!" Waddingham bellowed.

Edge scrambled to his feet and ran. When he reached the gravel verge of the road he dived into cover like a runner sliding head-first into home plate.

Another Russian loomed out of the flickering chaos, moving in short rushes. He had come from the fringe of trees, stalking prey. An explosion closer to the bridge lit Waddingham's kneeling outline in silhouette. As the Russian took aim he was plucked violently backwards, his helmet spinning in the air. The sudden roar of gunfire from so close by startled Waddingham. He spun wide-eyed and saw Kalina in the shadows.

"Get to the Wolverine!" Waddingham shouted again.

Edge and Kalina ran. They reached the Polish APC and scrambled behind its huge steel bulk for shelter. Russian bullets zinged off the hull, leaving bright silver scars in the metalwork.

"What are we doing here?" Edge gasped.

Waddingham climbed into the vehicle's darkened interior without answering. Kalina leaned her shoulder against the rear of the Wolverine and fired up the rise towards the enemy. The battlefield was enveloped in a moment of darkness and swirling smoke, but through the gloom shadows of running men ghosted.

"What are we looking for?" Edge repeated.

"This," Waddingham smiled with triumph. He was holding the CLU of an American Javelin missile system, and at his feet were two disposable launch tube assemblies, the black cannisters hung from thick shoulder straps.

The Javelin was a 'fire-and-forget' shoulder-launched anti-tank weapon that used an imaging infrared system to detect and lock onto enemy tanks at distances up to five thousand yards. Waddingham deftly began assembling the weapon's components. Edge ducked his head around the side of the Wolverine. The last remaining T-90 was on the crest of the rise, backlit by the flickering orange glow of a far-off explosion. The Russian tank began reversing up the slope, its turret traversing onto a Polish Wolverine that had been abandoned in the middle of the road.

"Kalina, find a radio! Any radio. You must get through to the TOC and tell command that the Russian mortars have been taken out. Tell them to attack across the bridge," Edge said.

Waddingham leaped down from the Wolverine and handed the spare missile tube to Edge. Kalina disappeared into the night. Waddingham crept to the corner of the Wolverine and settled the Javelin on his shoulder. He dropped to the ground, bracing his left leg forward, taking the weight of his body onto his right knee. He powered up the weapon and waited until he heard the battery hum to life.

"Take the shot!" Edge croaked.

Waddingham took a deep breath to settle himself. The night was ripped apart by the T-90's cannon firing. The muzzle flash leaped from the barrel like the fiery breath of a dragon and the night glowed with lurid orange light. The abandoned Wolverine, just fifty yards away from their position, disintegrated in a fireball of metal and flames. Shrapnel flew through the air like wind-driven rain, ripping through tree branches.

"Hurry, for Christ's sake!" Edge breathed.

Waddingham waited patiently. The T-90 became concealed behind a shroud of billowing grey smoke. The light behind the Russian tank flickered, died and then flared again as a fresh explosion fell in the distance. When the smoke drifted from the road, the T-90's turret began turning towards them – centering on the Wolverine where Edge and Waddingham sheltered.

"Jesus! Hurry up!" Edge hissed. "The tank is turning onto us. We're going to be killed you crazy bastard if you don't fire now. Fire!"

Still Waddingham waited. The T-90's turret continued to traverse. It seemed to Edge that he was staring down the open mouth of the tank's muzzle.

"Fire! For Christ's sake, fire!"

Waddingham locked on to the T-90. The tank was no more than three hundred paces away. Even in the gloomy glowing light Edge could see the tank's tracks in detail, see the rivets along the hull join, and see the camouflage net dangling from the length of its huge barrel.

"Fire!"

Waddingham squeezed the trigger. The Javelin leaped against his shoulder. The CLU ejected the missile from the launcher using a conventional rocket propellant. After a split-second delay the flight motor ignited, sending the missile skyward on a sparking tail of fire. Known as a 'curveball', the missile shot a hundred and fifty meters into the air before it began to plunge almost vertically onto the Russian tank. Waddingham and Edge were enveloped in a billow of smoke. Edge jumped to the left to clear his line of sight from the haze. The battlefield seemed to swim before his eyes. He saw the missile arrowing towards the T-90 and then the thin armor protecting the top of the tank was engulfed in a huge roiling wall of fire and black smoke.

The Russian tank blew apart. The shock of the massive explosion quivered the air and shook nearby trees. The vibration of the blast rumbled the earth beneath their feet. The rise in the road became shrouded in smoke, flickered by the light of the flames that engulfed the tank.

The Russian defenders had been reduced to fighting in shrunken, ragged pockets of resistance, crouched in their trenches by the road's crest that was blanketed in swirling smoke and lit up by tracer fire and explosions. Behind the fighting a couple of Iveco LMV's crowded with junior officers sped away, stealing cross-country into the night. One by one the Russian infantry still fighting began to abandon their positions. Some retreated and disappeared into the haze. A few – a very few – threw down their weapons and flung their arms in the air to surrender. Some fought on bravely. Others skulked away in the confusion and disappeared into the forest from where the Polish had launched their flank attack.

A sudden roaring engine made Edge turn. A Cavalry Stryker came racing across the bridge, its 50cal firing, hammering the air. Behind it followed a second vehicle and in the gloom of the night Edge saw more Strykers dashing forward. The Americans had won the bridge, the Russian armor defending the road had been destroyed, and the enemy's shattered infantry were in retreat.

Waddingham threw down the Javelin and snatched up his M4. Edge watched the silhouettes of three Russian soldiers melt into the forest fringe. He tapped Waddingham on the shoulder and pointed. "I'm going after those bastards."

Vince Waddingham nodded. "I'll come with you."

*

"Take the bridge!" Colonel Sutcliffe barked orders down the line. "Move! Move! Move!"

It was the order the column of Strykers had been worrying might never come. They had risked their lives to create a diversionary attack and they had paid heavily in vehicles and blood. The troopers inside each Stryker were angry and spoiling for revenge. The first vehicle jounced onto the bridge with its 50cal machine gun blazing a swathe of fury through the night. The commander and driver were tense, expecting at any moment to see death appear out of the darkness on a rocket's tail of fire and sparks. Behind the lead vehicle were two others, and behind them six more. The column was backed up for over a mile down the dark road.

The moment the lead Stryker reached the far side of the bridge the steel rear ramp came down and the infantry who were bottled up inside exploded through the opening. They dashed across the road, firing from the hip as they ran, eager to join the battle and come to grips with an enemy that had frustrated their advance for almost an entire day.

The troopers surged towards the crest of the road with a savage roar of vengeance in their throats. The shattered remnants of the Polish militia Company were swept along by the charge. Together the Allied troops overwhelmed the last of the defenders with sheer weight of numbers.

Some enemy infantry stubbornly refused to surrender. They fought from their trenches until the bitter end. A Russian Sergeant sprayed the night with machine gun fire until he ran out of ammunition, and then pulled the pin on a grenade and clutched it to his chest. A man fighting from a trench surrounded by sandbags was shot in the face when he rose from cover with a loaded RPG on his shoulder.

"Checkmate Six Romeo, this is Bull Six Actual," a Stryker Troop Commander radioed the TOC when his vehicle had joined the others on the far side of the bridge. "We have secured the crossing. Repeat. We have secured the crossing."

*

Edge slanted his pursuit through the forest, working an angle to intercept the Russians who had fled the fighting. He went cautiously, stepping high, watching the fall of each foot to minimize noise. Away from the fighting and within the embrace of the woods, the darkness quickly closed around him.

He dropped to a crouch and listened hard into the night. The sporadic flare of fighting from the bridge drowned out the sounds of any movement. He drew Vince Waddingham beside him and whispered in the dark.

"I think they're somewhere up ahead of us."

They pushed on, their ears tuned for abrupt noise, their weapons up and pulled into their shoulders, their eyes following the arc of the barrel as they moved. Waddingham drifted twenty yards to the left of Edge, maintaining their orientation through sense more than sight. The smell of smoke through the forest overpowered everything. Edge was anticipating a burst of Russian automatic fire, the sudden roar of bullets and a leaping tongue of flame that would presage his death. He heard nothing except the muted din of battle in the distance. A wisp of breeze rustled the upper branches of the trees then faded back to silence. Edge focused his attention until he could hear the thumping beat of his heart echo in his ears. The sound of every twig and dry leaf crackling underfoot sounded obscenely loud. He stepped into a small clearing lit by the night's ambient light, and waited. No shots rang out. No snarled voice cried a challenge in hatred or defiance.

Was he being watched? Were the Russians lying in ambush on the far side of the clearing, waiting for him to walk into their trap? He licked his lips. In his imagination every dark patch of shadow transformed into the silhouette of a Russian with his weapon raised; every faint sound manifested as a hoarse rasp of breath. His boot crunched down on a dead tree branch and he paused like a man who had trodden on a landmine. He swallowed hard and eased his foot back. Sweat ran in rivulets down his face and stung his eyes. He shivered and then let out a long silent sigh.

After ten tense minutes they found no sign of the enemy. It was as if the three Russians had melted into the darkness and vanished.

Edge let some of the tightness ease from his shoulders. The sounds of the battle had faded into the distance, coming in undulating snarls of frantic gunfire. He shuffled across to where Vince Waddingham stood and leaned his head close.

"They're gone," he conceded defeat. "We'll never find them now."

They had drifted north during their hunt. Edge turned due south, knowing eventually he would intersect the fire trail that would lead them back to the road. Waddingham followed in his wake, still alert, never allowing himself to relax.

A flare of white light appeared in the night.

"Down!" Edge hissed.

The two men dropped to the ground and lay unmoving for sixty seconds. The light remained constant; a twin beam that sliced through the night perhaps a hundred yards ahead of them, its narrow glow filtered by the intervening trees.

"Russians?" Waddingham whispered, lifting his head and peering through a gap in the foliage.

"Probably," Edge conceded. "Maybe the Ruskies had a couple of 4WD's parked in the forest in case they needed them for escape. We have to find out."

They crawled forward quickly, approaching the headlights from the side. As they drew closer, they heard muffled voices, speaking a foreign language in hushed but urgent tones. Edge saw the silhouettes of two men, moving back and forth across the lights. Then a third figure stepped into view. He leaned against Waddingham's ear and whispered.

"I can't understand a fucking word they're saying," Edge muttered. "But it seems like they're in a hurry. If we don't move soon we'll lose them."

He was about to come up onto his knees and take a firing position when Waddingham clamped a huge hand on his arm to stay the movement. He wriggled ten yards to his right, slithering like a snake, and stared intently. When he returned, and his face reappeared out of the darkness, he was smiling with cunning anticipation.

"That's not a 4WD, and they're not Russians," he whispered to Edge. "It's Major Nowakowski and a couple of his aides. They're standing in front of his Wolverine."

A figure moved across the headlights, gestured aggressively and then cursed. The sound of the man's voice carried clearly through the woods. Edge smiled savagely.

"I'm going to kill the bastard."

"What about the Russians?"

"Forget them," Edge hissed. "I want Nowakowski. The bastard has to pay for all the men who died today because of his cowardice."

Edge studied the tactical situation more closely. A narrow natural trail ran through the woods a few yards to their right, fringed by tall trees and dense clumps of bush. It might have once been a wildlife path, used by deer during the summer months. The ground was hard and worn smooth.

"I'm going to lie in ambush," Edge explained. "I want you to circle around to the far side of the Wolverine. In exactly seven minutes time I want you to open fire on the APC. Don't hit anyone! I just want you to frighten the life out of the bastards. Best guess is they'll run like cowards directly away from the attack. If they do, I'll be waiting for Nowakowski."

"Then what?"

"Then you follow the fire trail back to the road. I'll be along once I've finished doing what needs to be done."

Vince Waddingham said nothing. He ghosted away into the night, moving like a wraith to circle around the Wolverine and take up position. Edge watched the minutes and seconds tick down on the luminous dial of his wristwatch. With his free hand he reached around his body armor, past his spare M4 ammunition magazines, and felt for the M9 bayonet in its scabbard. He drew the wicked blade and absently tested the razor edge. Contempt and loathing came boiling up within him, his anger so fierce that it took all his self-will to restrain himself, to wait in the shadows patiently.

Even though he counted down the seconds and anticipated Waddingham's sudden fusillade, the sudden abrupt roar of gunfire still startled Edge. The bullets whanged off the steel hull of the Wolverine and ricocheted away into the trees. A tongue of flickering fiery flame lit up the night. There was a short split-second of silence, and then Waddingham fired again, this time spraying bullets into the canopy of tree branches overhead.

Edge heard the sudden unholy panic; the screams of startled fright from the men knotted around the Wolverine. He saw fleeting shapes flash across the headlights and then the sounds of desperate panting, crashing feet and gasps of terror.

He sank deeper down in the shadows and held his breath. Waddingham fired again and Edge suspected he had shifted his position, like a herder driving cattle. The clamor of gunfire sounded close and deafeningly loud. Then the dark night fell silent but for the sounds of scampering feet and hoarse ragged panting.

Edge drew himself tight, tensed his muscles like a coiled spring. He heard a crash of sound further away to his left, somewhere in the distance. It sounded like one of the men cannoned off a tree trunk in the dark and fell. Edge put the noise out of his mind and refocused. He could hear scurried footsteps approaching, the vibration of pounding feet coming up through the ground. Someone grunted, brushed clumsily past a bush and whimpered with fright. Then a voice cried out in fear and panic.

"Wait! I order you to wait for me!"

Nowakowski!

Edge felt the sudden surge of adrenalin and anticipation course through his veins. He clenched his fist around the handle of the M9 bayonet. His heart slammed against the cage of his ribs. He could feel the sinews of his muscles screw tight.

A figure ran past him in the night, running with long strides across the worn narrow path. Edge saw a slim silhouette flit past his hiding place and a moment later heavy pounding feet approached. They seemed leaden and dragging across the ground. He heard a breathless gasp and a labored grunt. Edge pounced.

He leaped from the hiding place and wrapped his arms around the second figure as it passed, bringing the man down like a lion hunting a deer. His weight and the shock of surprise collapsed the man's legs, and he crashed to the ground with Edge on top of him. The man screamed in fear; a high-pitched squeal of sheer terror. Edge punched the man hard in the face and then clamped his big hand over the open bleeding mouth.

"You gutless, filthy, cowardly bastard!" Edge spat. He could smell Major Nowakowski's rancid breath, smell the stench of fear ooze from his sweat-soaked body. Nowakowski reacted instinctively, galvanized by shock. He flailed his arms, trying to land punches. Edge swatted his hands away and punched him hard across the jaw.

The Polish Major went limp. His head lolled groggily to the side and a trickle of blood spilled from the corner of his mouth. Edge seized the Major by the collar and hauled his heavy bulk into the dark of the shadows.

"Your cowardice killed dozens of good, brave men today, you gutless bastard," Edge seethed through gritted teeth. The Major lay on his back in the dirt with Edge straddling his chest. Edge had the blade of the M9 bayonet pressed against the Polish officer's flabby neck flesh, barely able to restrain himself from plunging the blade through his heart, killing him outright. "They died because of you, you filthy fucking coward!"

"Is.. is that you, Edge?" Major Nowakowski babbled. His white face turned to find him in the darkness and he gave a sudden gasp of alarm. "Sergeant Edge? What are you doing?"

The pounding footsteps of the other fleeing men faded into the distance. The forest turned eerily silent. The only light came from the sprinkle of stars overhead, faded by drifting tendrils of smoke that twisted through the trees.

"Edge!" Nowakowski tried to pantomime a tone of arrogant command into his voice. "Damn you, get off me. I'll have you court-martialed for this I swear I –"

Edge punched the Major hard in the face. "You shut your fucking mouth," Edge seethed. "You don't have the guts to fight. All you're good for is sending other men to their deaths. Men like the troopers who attacked the bridge tonight. Men like the ones I led into battle while you sulked and cowered in the forest and let them get killed. So shut your mouth."

Nowakowski tried to wriggle from beneath Edge's weight. Edge pressed down until the wind was squeezed from the other man's lungs and he lay gasping and choking for breath.

The fight and bluster went from the Major and he became suddenly obsequious and fawning. "I.. I'm sorry, Edge. It wasn't my fault," he whined. "My officers. They – "

Edge pricked the tip of the bayonet into the soft flesh under the Major's chin and a trickle of warm blood ran down his arm. The Major squealed like a stuck pig and his eyes flew wide with terror. He flapped his hands in the dirt and broke into pathetic mewling sobs.

"Are you ready to die, you piece of shit? Are you ready to have your guts cut open and bleed to death? I'm told the pain is excruciating. I sincerely hope it is."

Edge raised the bayonet high and his snarling teeth flashed white in the darkness.

Major Nowakowski threw up his hands to shield his face. "No!"

Edge stilled his arm. Nowakowski licked his lips in nervous terror. "Anything. Anything you want."

Edge sneered. "You make me sick…"

"Anything!"

Edge slapped Nowakowski backhanded across the face. "Shut your fucking mouth and listen."

The Polish officer was weeping, his mouth wrought and blubbering.

"You're resigning your commission, immediately," Edge said. "I don't care what excuse you make, but you're leaving the Army tonight. You will retire from service and from public life. You will never command troops in the field again. Do you understand?"

Not trusting his voice, the Major swallowed hard and nodded jerky agreement.

"Say it!" Edge demanded.

"I agree!" Nowakowski almost shouted the words. "I give you my word. I will leave the Army tonight."

Edge let the tension go from his arm, then changed his mind. He steered the tip of the blade to the Major's face and held it just an inch from his eye. "If I ever see or hear your name again, I'll hunt you down. I will hunt you down and I will kill you in the worst way possible. I will torture you until you scream for mercy and then I'll slice your guts open and leave you for the vultures." Edge made sure the Major saw the cruel promise in his eyes, then got to his feet. Major Nowakowski stood unsteadily. He was covered in dirt and mud, his face pale as wax. He took a couple of tentative steps towards the Wolverine and his legs almost collapsed beneath him.

"Remember my promise, you disgusting piece of shit..." Edge called after him.

Edge stood amidst the shadows and waited until the Wolverine rumbled into life and disappeared along the fire trail. He waited until the headlights were blotted out by the forest and the sound of the revving engine had faded. Slowly he sheathed the M9 bayonet and let out a long ragged sigh of breath.

He felt deeply conflicted. He had wanted nothing more than to plunge his blade into the Polish officer's chest and kill him. It was the least the man deserved for all the chaos, pain and death he had caused. He looked about the shadows. He knew, despite his orders, that Vince Waddingham would be hidden somewhere close by.

"Did you hear that?" he asked softly.

The Scout Team Leader appeared out of the darkness a few feet away and gave Edge an admonishing smile. "People skills," he said in light-hearted rebuke. "I keep telling you – it's why no one likes you..."

*

The battle for the bridge had been won, but the fighting was not yet over.

At the crest of the road a pocket of Russians fought on against overwhelming odds, trapped and cut-off from retreat. With the scout Platoon's Strykers blockading the road north and the Cavalry and Polish surging over the bridge, the Russians had no other choice but to fight or surrender.

It was a brave, pitiful display of defiance that was quickly and brutally crushed. Fighting in the shadows of the two destroyed T-90's, the Russians were overwhelmed by a fusillade of 50cal machine gun fire.

When it was all over, an eerie silence descended across the battlefield. Without gunfire the blanket of darkness descended. Soldiers worked in the shadows to gather the dead and dying. The mutilated Russian corpses were piled in deep gruesome drifts by the side of the road. The American and Polish dead were transported from the field. Colonel Sutcliffe jumped the TOC to the far side of the bridge and a mobile field hospital was established. There were too many soldiers in need of urgent medical attention. The injured were left on stretchers in makeshift tents to await aid while medical staff weaved between the wounded dispensing temporary care. The surgeons worked through the night. Some of the wounded survived their ghastly injuries. Others did not.

The Americans moved quickly to secure the vital crossing. Stryker A1 IM-SHORAD's were positioned on the south side of the bridge on air defense duty. The vehicles, bristling with Hellfire and Stinger missiles, were the latest word in mobile air defense. They guarded the night sky against the threat of more Russian air attacks while on the ground, troopers armed with mobile Stinger systems climbed the crest of the ridge and set up air-defense outposts.

A Troop of Strykers raced two miles north along the road and established a perimeter while the rest of the Squadron's vehicles bivouacked for the night inside the forest. Men, bone-weary with fatigue and exhaustion, labored through the small hours of darkness to repair damage, re-load weapons and wash away the blood of battle.

A solemn, silent despair enveloped the battlefield. The soldiers went about their work with quiet, grim purpose. Some muttered silent prayers of thanks for surviving the hellish night. Others mourned the death of friends and comrades. It was a victory without celebration; a triumph but at terrible cost.

Russian prisoners were herded at gunpoint away into the night. They marched in ragged columns, hands on their heads, their steps bovine and leaden with defeat. The Americans had no contingency for POW's. The Cavalry was a flying column sent to harass the flank of the approaching Russian spearhead. It was one of the many unseen consequences of war that caused logistical nightmares.

In the night the rats came for the corpses and crows gathered to await the first light of dawn. The stench of death and blood hung like a pall. A fire broke out in the forest and a fresh storm of smoke boiled black into the sky. The blaze burned across the eastern ridge, but nobody bothered to contain its spread.

Edge and Waddingham emerged from the trees through a curtain of smoke and stared at the devastation. It was a scene from an apocalyptic nightmare; dark twisted skeletons of destroyed vehicles littered the shell-churned earth. Between the steel carcasses smoke-shrouded soldiers trudged like zombies.

Kalina emerged from the far side of the road; just another drab, weary figure spattered in mud and blood. Her shoulders were hunched, her expression inconsolably sad. She looked, Edge thought, to have aged through the night.

"I'm glad you are alive," Edge said.

Kalina nodded. "Many are not. Over half my militia Company were killed or injured, and I cannot find the Major – my father."

Edge said nothing.

Shaded headlight slits loomed out of the distant darkness and a few minutes later Lieutenant Colonel Marion Sutcliffe's command Stryker steered a weaving path across the wreckage-littered bridge. The Colonel stepped down from the vehicle gingerly, wincing from the effort. He stood and stared for long solemn minutes, overwhelmed by the vast devastation.

Edge and Waddingham left Kalina to attend to a wounded member of the militia. They drifted towards the bridge.

Colonel Sutcliffe recognized their mud-smeared faces. He nodded to acknowledge Edge's contribution.

"How did the Polish militia fight?" Colonel Sutcliffe asked. His voice was low. This was not a moment for loudly barked orders. Not here and not now – not after so many had died. The battlefield felt solemn as a cemetery, and subdued men's voices with somber respect.

"When they finally joined the battle, they were brave," Edge said.

"And the Russians?"

Edge shrugged. "Most chose to fight to the death rather than surrender. Every inch of ground we won had to be paid for with the blood of heroes. If what happened here is a fair indication of the enemy's morale and fighting abilities, this is going to be a long and costly war."

Vince Waddingham nodded to confirm Edge's assessment, but then a cocky smile drifted to his lips. "The Russians should have defended with elite troops, sir. They forgot the golden rule of war. *If you ain't Cav, you ain't shit.*"

Facebook: https://www.facebook.com/NickRyanWW3
Website: https://www.worldwar3timeline.com

Acknowledgements:

The greatest thrill of writing, for me, is the opportunity to research the subject matter and to work with military, political and historical experts from around the world. I had a lot of help researching this book from the following groups and people. I am forever grateful for their willing enthusiasm and cooperation. Any remaining technical errors are mine.

Randy Harris

Randy is a retired Cavalry Major with more than 43 years experience in the US Army and Army National Guard. Randy was instrumental in helping me to understand the structure of a Cavalry Squadron and all its components.

NATO enhanced Forward Presence Battle Group Poland

The Public Affairs folks at the NATO eFP in Poland were helpful explaining a broad overview of the Bemowo Piskie training area and the role of certain buildings within the facility.

Dion Walker Sr.

Sergeant First Class (Retired) Dion Walker Sr, served 21 proud years in the US Army with deployments during Operation Desert Shield/Storm, Operation Intrinsic Action and Operation Iraqi Freedom. For 17 years he was a tanker in several Armor Battalions and Cavalry Squadrons before spending 4 years as an MGS (Stryker Mobile Gun System) Platoon Sergeant in a Stryker Infantry Company.

More than anyone else, Dion's advice and knowledge made this novel possible and I am forever in his debt for his enthusiastic support, his prompt help with research questions and his willingness to help make each scene as authentic as possible.

Major John Ambelang, Public Affairs Officer, 2d Cavalry Regiment

Major Ambelang was a great help while I was plotting and conducting preliminary research for the novel, providing clarification and some details about the organizational structure of a US Cavalry Squadron.

Jill Blasy:

Jill has the editorial eye of an eagle! I trust Jill to read every manuscript, picking up typographical errors, missing commas, and for her general 'sense' of the book. Jill has been a great friend and a valuable part of my team for several years.

Jan Wade:

Jan is my Personal Assistant and an indispensable part of my team. She is a thoughtful, thorough, professional and persistent pleasure to work with. Chances are, if you're reading this book, it's due to Jan's engaging marketing and promotional efforts.

Printed in Great Britain
by Amazon